"You carefully _differences be_

Luke continued, "How I was nothing but a poor, crude, undereducated tramp, while you were cultured, well educated, well paid and, after that long shower, no doubt well cleansed. No dirt under your fingernails, right, lawyer lady?"

"I never made any such comparisons," J.J. exclaimed.

"Not in so many words, but even a dumb cowboy could guess what you were thinking."

"I didn't have to guess what you were thinking, did I? You told me. You wanted a wife whom you expected to wear jeans, but not the pants in the family. You wanted a woman to cook your meals, wash your socks, warm your bed and raise your children. You didn't want a wife—you wanted an unpaid servant!"

"I wanted a woman," he said coldly, "who wanted a man. I don't know what the hell you wanted."

Dear Reader,

Welcome to the next book in our exciting showcase series for 1997! Once again we're delighted to bring you a specially chosen story we know you're going to enjoy, again and again...

Authors you'll treasure, books you'll want to keep!

This month's recommended reading is
Do You Take This Cowboy? by Jeanne Allan. Find out what happens when headstrong cowboy Luke Remington meets J.J. O'Brien, the hot city lawyer.... Our SIMPLY THE BEST novel for October will be *No Wife Required!* by Rebecca Winters (#3477).

Happy Reading!

The Editors,
Harlequin Romance

Do You Take This Cowboy?

Jeanne Allan

Harlequin Books

TORONTO • NEW YORK • LONDON
AMSTERDAM • PARIS • SYDNEY • HAMBURG
STOCKHOLM • ATHENS • TOKYO • MILAN
MADRID • WARSAW • BUDAPEST • AUCKLAND

ISBN 0-373-03471-7

DO YOU TAKE THIS COWBOY?

First North American Publication 1997.

Copyright © 1997 by Jeanne Allan.

All rights reserved. Except for use in any review, the reproduction or utilization of this work in whole or in part in any form by any electronic, mechanical or other means, now known or hereafter invented, including xerography, photocopying and recording, or in any information storage or retrieval system, is forbidden without the written permission of the publisher, Harlequin Enterprises Limited, 225 Duncan Mill Road, Don Mills, Ontario, Canada M3B 3K9.

All characters in this book have no existence outside the imagination of the author and have no relation whatsoever to anyone bearing the same name or names. They are not even distantly inspired by any individual known or unknown to the author, and all incidents are pure invention.

This edition published by arrangement with Harlequin Books S.A.

® and TM are trademarks of the publisher. Trademarks indicated with ® are registered in the United States Patent and Trademark Office, the Canadian Trade Marks Office and in other countries.

Printed in U.S.A.

CHAPTER ONE

J.J. HAD never seen a more beautiful woman. Envy, no less intense for being unexpected and totally irrational, slammed her in the stomach. The painting, simply titled Her Life, portrayed the pioneer woman hanging her washing on a sagging clothesline. Near the woman a pair of toddlers played in a small garden patch, a baby slept in a cradle, a pie cooled in an open window and a shotgun leaned against the door of a small sod house. The signs of human activity occupied less than one-quarter of the painting while a flat, bleached sky and parched, treeless plain filled the rest. J.J. wondered if the artist had mounted the watercolor on a slab of old barn wood rather than frame it to symbolize the sense the pioneers must have had of vast, never-ending prairie and sky.

The dull, nearly monochromatic watercolor presented an eloquent portrayal of hardship, loneliness and despair until one noticed the tiny daubs of color. Dimly visible in the background a man guiding a wooden plow behind a plodding horse wore a barn red bandanna around his neck. Near the house a single garish pink rose bloomed on a scraggly bush. The artist had cleverly used the two splashes of color to guide the viewer to the faded indigo blue of the woman's bonnet hanging down her back as she lifted her face to the sky. The woman's sun-and-wind-ravaged face shone with strength, courage and hope.

J.J. debated mentioning the painting to Burton. He was too well mannered to gloat, but after her fuss about being dragged down near Larimer Square in Denver to the gallery opening on her birthday, he'd be entitled to a passing moment of satisfaction at hearing she'd seen at least one picture she liked. Not that she could explain the effect the watercolor had had on her.

Chattering self-importantly about the artist's technique and minimalist color sense, a group of people crowded around J.J. Not wanting their pretentious opinions to taint her instinctive reaction to the watercolor, J.J. moved on through the gallery. Puzzling over her unexpected response to the watercolor, she barely noticed the other paintings hanging on the walls.

Suddenly the sensation of being watched pricked the base of her spine. In the way a wild animal recognizes her mate, she sensed him before he spoke.

"Hello, O'Brien."

J.J. turned slowly. Her gaze collided with a red silk tie littered with whitened cattle skulls. She blinked and shuddered. Her gaze crawled upward past the blunted point of the cleft chin, dark with its habitual five-o'clock shadow, and halted in fascination at the tiniest twitch at the corner of the lips. They were ordinary lips; certainly no reason for her insides to pitch and roll.

The lips moved. "The tie was a gift." Amusement rippled through his deep voice. "You're looking good, O'Brien. In spite of that feed sack you're wearing."

She forced herself to meet Luke Remington's eyes. Hazel eyes that combined gray-brown with blue in a thousand different ways depending on his mood. She'd told him once his eyes were the color of her brother's favorite agate marble. He'd laughed and said the color made him think of a pond filled with muddy silt. Now she said, "Hello, cowboy. No time no see," with just the right tone of airy nonchalance. He'd never know her pulse threatened to burst through her skin.

He'd changed little since she'd seen him a year ago. Then she'd foolishly considered him the handsomest man ever to cross her path. Her infatuation conquered, she thought his ears stuck out a little from his head. He'd never tame the wave above his left temple. He wasn't handsome. He was heart-stoppingly male.

J.J. wrapped her fingers tightly around the handle of her leather briefcase, thrusting treacherous memories back into their deep hiding place before he read them in her eyes. No one else had ever come close to reading her the way he had. Or so she'd thought. She smiled, a practiced, professional smile. "What are you doing here?"

"That." The tanned skin at the corners of his eyes crinkled, and Luke nodded to the wall behind her. "I guess it's not such a good likeness. You didn't recognize me."

J.J. whirled to face the oil painting she'd been standing blindly in front of. Dismay flooded through her. Why couldn't she have stopped in front of any other painting? Tilting her head, she stared critically at the painting, searching for something dismissive to say.

A cowhand and his horse stood wearily, their dirty, sweat-covered bodies sagging. J.J. concentrated on the man's face. Luke's face. Satisfaction overrode the weariness. The air of a job well done. The same feeling she had after she'd won a particularly difficult case. The satisfaction a person could only earn. Not meaning to, she asked abruptly, "Why are you looking so pleased with yourself?" Then she saw the tiny calf sprawled across the saddle and had to smile. "You saved him." She turned. Luke's gaze caressed her face. Remembered pleasure shimmered over her skin.

"You cut your hair." He cocked his head to one side. "I like it. Makes you look sexy as hell."

J.J. arched a haughty brow. Her stylist cut her medium gray-brown hair chin-length to curve slightly under in a severe businesslike style. "It's practical."

His half smile told her how little he thought of her claim. A lazy warmth stirred in the back of his eyes. "Very sexy." He sent a provocative gaze crawling the length of her body. "I'll bet a year's wages you're wearing slinky silk underwear under that horse blanket," he drawled.

"It's not a horse blanket." If she were a better liar, she'd tell him he'd loose his bet.

"There you are, J.J. I lost you in the crowd. Ready to go eat?" Burton lightly touched her arm.

Gratefully J.J. swung around to smile at him. "Yes."

"Ah, you've forgiven me for persuading you to attend the opening," Burton teased. His gaze slid beyond her, touching first on the painting, then on Luke. "I don't believe we've met. I'm Burton Alexander. That's you in the painting, isn't it?"

"It's me," Luke agreed.

The two men couldn't have presented a greater contrast. Burton, wearing a conservatively cut, charcoal pinstriped suit, white-on-white striped button-down shirt and red Italian foulard tie, looked the very successful lawyer he was. If he envied Luke's four-inch height advantage, tanned, rugged good looks, and broad-shouldered, lean-hipped physique clad in jeans, blue denim shirt and tweed sport coat, Burton managed to keep any trace of that envy from showing. Burton probably didn't even notice Luke's aura of sex appeal, which had every woman in range preening and wishing she were the focus of all that raw masculinity.

"Are you a model?" Burton asked.

Luke laughed. "No. Harve wanted to paint some spring ranch scenes, so he stayed with us for a couple of weeks last year." He extended his hand, introducing himself. "Luke Remington."

Burton shook hands. "Remington," he repeated, his brow wrinkling. "You aren't—"

"Yes, he is." J.J. confirmed Burton's obvious surmise. "Isn't this an amusing birthday surprise? My husband and the man I'm going to marry running into each other like this. What are the odds?"

*   *   *

Burton looked around the restaurant in the area of lower downtown Denver known as LoDo. "I should have canceled these reservations. I'm sure you would have preferred a T-bone or something."

"Eye-talian's okay," Luke assured him. "I can always order spaghetti. I reckon I know what that is."

"I shouldn't have ordered wine," Burton continued. "You probably prefer beer."

"Yeah, us beer-guzzling cowboys ain't got much of them palates," Luke pronounced it *pah-lates,* "for fancy stuff."

The sarcasm found its mark, and Burton's face reddened. The appearance of a waiter to take their orders gave the older man time to consider his words. "I apologize for my idiotic remarks. I didn't mean, well, this is a little awkward, isn't it?"

His rare loss of composure underlined how awkward. For the first time since J.J. had known him, Burton Alexander's brilliant legal mind and famous unflappable demeanor had deserted him. Of course, he'd never before dined with the husband of his future wife. Not that he hadn't brought the uncomfortable situation on himself by inviting Luke Remington to join them for dinner. J.J. had always admired Burton's impeccable manners. If only certain others shared them. She glared across the table at her husband. "Any gentleman with a smidgen of acquaintance with proper etiquette would have politely declined Burton's rhetorical invitation."

"Goldarn, O'Brien, I wish you wouldn't mix me up with all them big words. If you're talking manners, I took off my hat, and I *shure* mean to eat without usin' my fingers." He gave her a soulful, accusing look. "If you rightly remember, lawyer lady, I ain't had the benefit of all your fancy schoolin'."

"You might remember I wasn't born yesterday," J.J. said, "so stop that ridiculous corn pone act right now."

"I thought the simple, down-to-earth quality about me is what attracted you," Luke drawled.

"Why do you call her O'Brien?" Burton asked quickly.

"J.J. ain't no kind of name for a woman like O'Brien."

"If you say 'ain't' one more time," J.J. snapped, "I am going to throw my Caesar salad at you."

Satisfaction gleamed briefly in Luke's eyes before he turned to Burton. "So you and O'Brien plan on getting hitched."

"After she gets her divorce, yes," Burton said cautiously.

"I wondered if she'd remembered that little detail." A feral grin curved Luke's mouth. "I suppose that's why you invited me to dinner. To soften me up for a divorce."

"I thought dinner would be an excellent opportunity for us to become acquainted. I assume a divorce between you and J.J. is a mere formality."

Luke gave Burton a cool, assessing look. "Why would you assume that?"

"You've been separated for a year."

"Didn't our vows say something about as long as we both lived?" Luke asked J.J.

"I remember very little of our so-called wedding, including the vows," J.J. said in a forbidding voice.

Luke's grin returned. "I guess we were in too big a hurry to get back to your place to remember much of anything about our wedding. In a hurry to get to bed," he added, in case Burton needed a picture painted. "I offered to buy her a big, fancy wedding lunch, but O'Brien wouldn't even stop for that."

Because she'd been worried he didn't have that kind of money. A suspicion she hadn't voiced then, and wasn't about to voice now. In spite of Luke's provocative comments. "Burton is less interested in our wedding than in our divorce."

"I have a little interest in that subject myself."

"Then you'll raise no objection to meeting in my office on Monday so we can discuss some of the details," J.J. said.

Luke took his time swallowing some wine. "No."

"Good." The empty feeling in the pit of her stomach came from delaying dinner so they could attend the gallery opening. She picked up her wineglass and saluted Luke. "Here's to a friendly, amicable divorce."

Luke set down his glass and leaned back against his chair. "I meant no, I won't go to your office Monday and discuss a divorce."

Burton said, "If Monday is inconvenient, we can—"

"What's inconvenient is a divorce." Nothing about Luke Remington's flat statement indicated he was kidding.

J.J. banged her wineglass down on the table. "Our marriage is inconvenient."

Luke looked from her to Burton and back again. He raised an insulting eyebrow. "Doesn't seem to be."

"J.J. has always behaved with the utmost propriety. Her conduct has been honorable throughout our acquaintanceship." Burton added dryly, "In case I've used words of too many syllables for you, Mr. Remington, I'll state this simply. J.J. has never slept with me. She refuses to do so until she obtains a decree of Dissolution of Marriage."

"Why not, O'Brien?"

"It has nothing to do with you." Luke had been the first and only man in her bed. J.J. drew on the tablecloth with her fork handle, and repeated the explanation she'd given Burton. "Burton has an adolescent daughter. When I'm her stepmother, I don't want to be in the position of counseling Carrie against premarital sex when she would be bound to know if her father and I engaged in it."

She could have added, everything in her screamed against an adulterous relationship; instead she changed the subject. "What do you mean a divorce is inconvenient? We agreed we were totally incompatible."

His casual comments that morning a year ago about her moving had caught her totally by surprise. She'd assumed they'd live in Denver where she worked for a prominent law firm earning good money with excellent prospects for earning better. She'd purchased her town house six months earlier. As a homeowner and the larger wage earner, never once had it occurred to her he'd expect her to pull up stakes and follow him to the boondocks. She'd expected Luke to look for employment in Denver.

The stunning realization he'd been thinking along totally different lines, making totally different assumptions had forced her to face reality. "We agreed we'd be better off facing the truth that we'd been foolishly impulsive. We agreed dissolving the marriage made more sense than deceiving ourselves into thinking we could make it work."

They'd been kidding themselves if they thought the emotion between them was love. People in love asked questions, made plans. She knew he liked hot, buttered popcorn, hated flavored coffee and moved with a slow indolence, which could disappear at a second's notice. He sang off-key in the shower. When he showered alone. He'd been an imaginative, satisfying lover. She had no idea how he'd expected to support them if she abandoned the practice of law.

"I knew something was up when you spent over an hour in the shower that Monday morning," Luke said. "You came out of the bathroom armored from head to toe in a heavy bathrobe and announced you'd changed your mind. You carefully pointed out the differences between us. How I was nothing but a poor, crude, undereducated saddle tramp while you were cultured, well educated, well paid, and after that long shower, no doubt well cleansed. No dirt under your fingernails, right, lawyer lady?''

J.J. knew her face matched the tomato on her plate. ''I never made any such comparisons.''

''Not in so many words, but even a dumb cowboy could guess what you were thinking.''

''I didn't have to guess what you were thinking, did I? You told me. You wanted a wife who worked side by side with her husband. A wife whom you expected to wear jeans, but not the pants in the family. You wanted a woman to cook your meals, wash your socks, warm your bed and raise your children. You didn't want a wife—you wanted an unpaid servant.''

''I wanted a woman,'' he said coldly, ''who wanted a man. I don't know what the hell you wanted. You had a great time slumming for a week, playing house with a big, bad cowboy. Then reality slapped you in the face, and you panicked at the thought of moving to North Park.''

''I didn't panic. I came to my senses. One of us had to be pragmatic.''

Luke snorted. ''Pragmatic, hell. You were plain chicken.''

''We're getting away from the point,'' Burton said. ''Why would a divorce inconvenience you, Mr. Remington?''

''Call me Luke. If we're going to share a wife, we ought to be on a first-name basis.''

''You are not going to share me.''

''Perhaps it would be best if we left O'Brien out of this discussion. Women tend to get so emotionally tied up in a situation, it's impossible for them to reduce a thing to its lowest common denominator.''

''I'm not sure I follow you, Remington.''

The barest hint of a mocking smile registered Luke's appreciation of Burton refusing to use his first name.

"O'Brien wants to be the man in the family, so let's talk alimony."

Shock surged through J.J.'s veins. "Alimony! I'm not going to pay you one thin dime." How could she ever have thought she loved this man? "No judge in the world would order me to pay alimony to an able-bodied man."

"Well, now, about that able-bodied business," he drawled. "I might have pulled or strained something the day I met you."

"Of all the outrageous lies!"

"And there's, what do they call it? Loss of consortium?" Luke shook his head sadly. "Almost a week of unmitigated bliss, and then, boom, nothing. Being cut off like that can cause intense physical and psychological damage to a man."

"Unmitigated bliss." J.J. ground her teeth. "The only thing unmitigated is your gall."

"You mean you didn't feel our marriage was a pure and sacred union of two minds? You didn't feel two hearts beating as one?"

"The only thing between us was sex," J.J. was driven to say, "and you know it."

Luke grinned wickedly. "So you do remember a few things about our marriage."

Before she could explode, Burton intervened. "Maybe we ought to hear what he has to say, J.J. I'm sure we can negotiate a settlement agreeable to all of us. Put your offer on the table, Remington."

"I'm not going to negotiate anything with him." She'd once thought he loved her. Though he'd never said so.

"Let's start with me saving O'Brien's life. That ought to be worth something to you, Alexander."

"You want payment for that?" J.J. gasped. "That's the most despicable thing you've said so far."

"I didn't realize you'd saved J.J.'s life," Burton said.

"See, O'Brien. It makes a difference to your boy-friend. How much is she worth to you?" he asked Burton.

"J.J. is above price."

"Thank you, Burton."

"And he hasn't even slept with you. Imagine how your value will go up then."

"That does it. I'd hoped we could settle this like two civilized people, but if you want to fight this divorce action, cowboy, go ahead and fight. By the time I get through with you, you'll feel as if every cow in North Park has stomped on you."

"Easy, J.J. There's no need to act in haste. If you'll allow me to act as your lawyer—"

"I don't need a lawyer, Burton. I *am* a lawyer."

"I didn't know about O'Brien's temper, did you, Alexander? She's kinda cute when she's mad, isn't she?"

An underlying tone she couldn't identify in Luke's voice brought J.J. up short. The suspicion took root that Luke was deliberately baiting her. She forced herself to speak in an admirably steady voice. "What is it you want?"

Luke stopped eating and stared thoughtfully at her for a long time. "You mentioned," he finally said, "something that morning about bright prospects." A chilling smile slowly curved his lips. "What's it worth to you to get rid of me? To fix it so our paths never again cross?"

Bitter acid chewed J.J.'s stomach. She'd married this man, slept with him and planned to spend the rest of her life with him. She'd thought she knew him. She hadn't known him at all.

He'd come barreling from out of nowhere, shoving her aside as he grabbed the toddler she'd paused to smile at. It happened so fast she didn't even have time to yell. One second J.J. was bending over a little girl in her stroller; the next she was flying through the air. The action seemed to occur in slow motion—shock, disbelief, hearing the commotion around her, knowing she was going to fall and knowing she could do nothing to catch herself. Her bottom had not yet hit the ground when a huge brown horse thundered past, his deadly hooves slashing down the wide aisle.

As J.J. sat stunned, the mother dashed over to grab her child and tearfully thank Luke. By the time Luke turned to J.J., she'd realized what had happened. The horse had broken loose from his handlers and dashed for freedom. Totally oblivious to their danger, J.J. and the little girl, whose mother had wandered a few steps away to pet another horse, stood in the runaway's path. If Luke hadn't seen the danger and acted instantaneously, both J.J. and the child might have been seriously maimed, if not killed.

Before J.J. could thank Luke, he'd extended a helping hand, given her a rueful smile and apologized. The twinkle in his eyes had directed J.J.'s attention behind her. She'd landed in a large, steaming pile of what her dad called "horse apples." J.J. never knew if it was the twinkling eyes, the rueful smile, or the incongruity of Luke apologizing for soiling her skirt when he'd saved her life, but she'd laughed until tears came. Five days later, the next Wednesday, they'd gotten married. The following Monday they'd agreed to a separation.

And not once in that time had J.J. entertained even the slightest notion that one day Luke Remington would try to extort money from her. A sense of loss engulfed her. She'd given herself to this man. Thought she'd loved him. She hadn't. Infatuation, that's all it had been. Brought on by gratitude plus the fact Luke Remington had more than his fair share of sex appeal. She'd been foolishly impulsive, but sometimes, at night, bittersweet memories of that week filled her dreams. No more. Luke watched her, waiting for her answer. J.J. swallowed hard against the nausea rising in her throat. "How much did you have in mind?"

"Three weeks."

J.J. blinked in confusion. "Three weeks of what? My draw from the firm?"

"You," Luke said softly. "Three weeks of you." He took a bite of crusty bread, his white teeth crunching savagely.

Burton choked on his wine. "Now just a minute, Remington."

"You're crazy," J.J. said flatly.

Luke looked at her, a small, humorless smile playing at the corners of his mouth. "Not crazy. Mad. As in seriously annoyed."

"You have nothing to be annoyed about."

"Maybe I didn't like being kicked out."

"We've been separated for a year," J.J. said, "and you've made no effort to contact me in that time."

"I hope you didn't expect me to come crawling on my hands and knees to Denver, begging you to take me in."

"Of course not. And I don't believe you want me back."

"Who said I wanted you back?"

"You did," J.J. said through clenched teeth. "You said you wanted me for three weeks. Forget it. Take a cold shower."

"You think I meant...?" Luke laughed mockingly. "I said I was annoyed, not desperate for sex. No matter how good it was between us." He paused. "And it was very, very good."

J.J.'s face flamed. She felt Burton, who'd remained silent through the interchange, shift beside her. She didn't need him to handle this for her. Before he could intercede, she spoke quickly. "Quit playing games, Luke, and tell me exactly what you're after."

"One year ago I married you, planning to share my life with you. Oddly enough, I thought you planned to share your life with me, but fancy lawyer ladies don't share their lives with riffraff, do they?"

"I'm sorry if I hurt your pride, but I'm not going to give you one thin dime."

Burton cleared his throat.

"No, Burton, I am not. I'm going to initiate divorce proceedings tomorrow, and there is nothing Luke Remington can do to stop me."

"Maybe not stop you," Luke said, "but I can sure slow the process down. Not to mention spice it up. I'm willing to bet you've bested more than one lawyer in Denver who'd be thrilled to represent me. We could come up with enough writs, habeas corpuses, court orders or other legal mumbo jumbo to create a judicial mine field between you and your holy grail. It would make for nice, juicy reading in the newspapers, don't you think, lawyer lady?"

"I'm sure you're prepared to propose an alternative, Remington," Burton said.

"As it happens, I am." Luke looked steadily at J.J. "You come back with me, spend three weeks at my place."

"No," she said.

"Scared?"

"I'm not—"

"Sure you are," Luke said coolly. "You're nothing but a canary yellow chicken masquerading as a tough guy. Everybody here might buy your act, but you're terrified real people would spot what a fake you are."

"You can't challenge me into taking up your insane proposition." J.J. had faced far more formidable opponents in court to fall into Luke's flimsy trap.

Luke laughed shortly. "Three weeks," he repeated. "Then I'll sign any divorce papers you stick in front of me. Hell, when you marry Alexander, I'll even give away the bride."

*　　*　　*

"Happy birthday to me," J.J. said bitterly as she paced back and forth across the living room of her Denver town house. "If you hadn't insisted we go to that stupid opening... I hate Western art. It was as clichéd as I feared it would be." No doubt the glass of champagne she'd drunk on arrival at the gallery had everything to do with her momentary weakness in front of the water-color of the pioneer woman. The champagne or hunger pangs. She'd lost her appetite soon enough.

"The gallery's owners are clients," Burton reminded her again. "I had to make an appearance."

"I don't know why they had to have the opening during the stock show." J.J. continued to pace.

Burton didn't bother to point out the obvious connection between the National Western Stock Show and Western art. They both knew her anger and frustration weren't directed toward the gallery opening. "You never told me Remington saved your life."

"He was playing hero and pushed me out of the way of a runaway horse at the stock show last year." She didn't want to be reminded of her obligation.

"What were you doing at the stock show? You're the last person I'd expect to be at a rodeo."

"Not the rodeo. I was in one of the barns or something. You know how the firm feels about us doing pro bono work." At his nod she continued, "I was there interviewing a potential witness in a domestic violence case." She made a face. "That was when I was still assigned all the cases with a woman's angle."

"Did you ever consider you were assigned those cases because you did such a superb job handling them?"

"C'mon, Burton, we both know I'm the token woman in the firm, hard as it is to believe in this day and age. The partners still think women ought to be kept barefoot and pregnant." Her churning emotions wouldn't allow her to stand still.

Burton laughed. "I don't think they're quite that bad.

And you might remember you're speaking to one of the partners."

"I remember. I'll be grateful to you until the day I die for persuading the others to give me a chance to prove I could stand up to the big boys in court."

"Is that why you agreed to marry me? Gratitude?"

J.J.'s pacing came to an abrupt halt, and she whirled to face Burton. "Of course not. And before you ask, I didn't agree to marry you to advance my career, either. I'm extremely fond of you and Carrie, and I know you're starting to feel out of your depth with Carrie on the brink of womanhood. I want to help you. I hope I can make life a little easier for both of you."

"You don't mention love."

After a long moment, J.J. said, "You've never mentioned love before. I thought you preferred it that way. I know you wouldn't remarry if it weren't for Carrie. I assumed you didn't want the burden of another woman loving you when you felt you couldn't return her love."

"Are you in love with me, J.J.?"

"I care for you very much."

Outside her curtained windows, the scream of emergency vehicles tore through the night. Burton seemed not to hear the sirens as he stared at a spot on the wall beyond J.J. "When Caroline died of ovarian cancer, I wanted to die, too, but I couldn't. I had Carrie."

"Caroline was a beautiful person. You and Carrie must miss her terribly." J.J. hesitated. "I want Carrie and me to be good friends. I don't intend to take the place of her mother."

"Carrie wants you for her stepmother." Looking down at his folded hands, Burton said somberly, "I don't think Carrie and I could deal with losing another wife and mother."

"You're not going to lose me. Once we're married, I'm sticking to you two like glue."

"I imagine Remington thought you'd stick with him."

"Burton, he expected me to give up everything. Sell my house, quit being a lawyer, go off to the boonies where all I'd be is his housekeeper and lover. I didn't go to college for six years and work all those extra hours at the office to toss it all away for a man who doesn't own much more than a saddle."

"You've kept your marriage a secret. I didn't even know you were married until I asked you to marry me. Even then you told me little, and I didn't want to probe." He looked at her with unblinking eyes. "I've known you since you joined our firm four years ago, J.J. You are not a woman of impulse, yet you married Luke Remington after knowing him less than one week."

"In a moment of insanity. I was a fool, okay? Can't we leave it at that?"

"I want you to enter into our marriage absolutely certain of what you're doing."

"I am absolutely certain." She stepped nearer, willing him to believe her. "Years ago I decided I wanted to be a successful top corporate lawyer. I thought I'd have to forego a husband and children, but with you and Carrie I'll have everything."

"Everything," Burton repeated gravely. He contemplated her as she stood in front of him. "I met Caroline in college. The first day she walked into speech class I decided to ask her out. I was still gathering my courage several weeks later when she gave a wonderful speech on women's rights. After class I complimented her. She gave me a smile so filled with a mixture of gratitude and triumph that right then and there I blurted out I intended to marry her."

J.J. smiled gently at Burton. "What did she say?"

"She said it was all right with her, but she hated to play bridge, she wanted six kids and she expected to live in a big house." He looked into space. "The powers that be saw fit to bless us only with Carrie, but at least Caroline had her big house, and we never played a game of bridge during our entire marriage.'' His gaze returned to J.J. "I loved her deeply."

"I don't expect that kind of love," J.J. said quietly.

"Don't you see what I'm getting at? Love at first sight might be a cliché, but with Caroline and I, it happened. And it lasted. Sure, we disagreed on hundreds of things, and we fought, but we worked things out because we loved each other."

J.J. gave him a confident smile. "You and I disagree on very little."

"J.J.—" Burton reached out and pulled her down beside him on the sofa "—I know you. You wouldn't have married Remington if you didn't love him."

"But that's exactly what I did do." She tried to explain. "Focusing so intently on my studies and then on work, wanting so desperately to succeed, I had no time for the usual dating scene. I was pretty naive. Luke was the first attractive man to come along who didn't seem intimidated or challenged by my being a lawyer. He could have had any woman at the stock show, and he chose me." She smiled crookedly. "I thought he admired my mind. I fell pretty hard. Now I know what I felt was physical attraction, not love."

Burton didn't look at her. "Tonight, seeing you two together... I don't think you've resolved your first marriage."

"A divorce will resolve it."

Burton shook his head. "I'm not so certain of that." He clasped J.J.'s hands in his. "I want you to accept his invitation to spend three weeks with him."

"I can't take off from work for three weeks."

"I'll take care of the arrangements. You don't have any major cases on the calendar right now. I can shift or postpone your other clients and appointments."

"I'm not going to pander to Luke Remington's injured ego. He can hire every lawyer in Denver, but he has nothing he can hold over my head.''

"I'm not asking you to go because it would facilitate your divorce, J.J.'' Burton's grip tightened around her hand. ''I'm asking because I want you to be sure of what you're doing.''

"I am sure. I want to marry you, Burton.''

"I don't want…'' He paused, then reworded what he was about to say, "I will not marry a woman who might be in love with another man.'' Ignoring her sputtering denial, Burton eyed her steadily. "When you say 'I do,' I want both of us to be absolutely, positively certain you're not in love with Luke Remington.''

CHAPTER TWO

"SULK ALL you want, O'Brien, but you're staying three weeks." The light amusement in Luke Remington's voice underscored his triumph.

J.J. continued to stare out the side window. Most of her life had been spent competing with men who liked to rub it in when they won. Especially if the loser was a woman. Luke Remington could crow and flex all the muscles he wanted. She hadn't come because of any stupid threats he'd made.

Since picking up J.J. and her luggage, Luke had concentrated on the heavy traffic weaving its way west out of Denver on I-70. The wind had come up around Idaho Springs, and when J.J. looked in the large mirror outside the passenger side of Luke's dirty, beat-up pickup, she saw the horse trailer behind them rocking slightly as gusts buffeted it. She wondered if horses suffered from motion sickness. Asking meant speaking to Luke. She wasn't that interested.

Bare aspens, icicles linking eaves to snowbanks and the snow-packed icy road snaking over Berthoud Pass told of a land firmly gripped by winter. Blowing snow blurred the line between cloudless blue sky and mountain peaks. Cut snowbanks, almost the height of the truck, wore stripes of brown and white. A tiny white whirlwind spun across the highway. J.J. shivered in spite of the intense January sun heating up the pickup's interior.

Luke had insisted her small car wasn't up to ranch living. She'd be a virtual prisoner for three weeks. An eternity.

"I'd ask if you ever got around to skiing Winter Park, but I'm sure you avoided this area like the plague," he said.

Her jaw stayed locked. Huge metallic snowflakes hung from light poles along the main street of the ski town. Luke knew she'd planned to go skiing with friends last year the weekend after he'd played hero. He also knew she'd sent regrets. She'd long ago lost track of how many times she'd cursed herself for that particular decision. And others. If only she hadn't been in the stock barn at that particular moment. If she hadn't stopped to talk to the little girl...

In Fraser, red-and-white bands wrapped the light poles to resemble candy canes. She'd heard the small town was the icebox of the U.S. No doubt Luke lived in an uninsulated, beat-up old house trailer. J.J. burrowed deeper into her down coat.

"If you're cold, O'Brien, I can turn on the heater."

She didn't bother to acknowledge his concession to the loser. He'd only made it to point out the sissy little woman couldn't take the cold. Unlike tough and macho Luke Remington. Besides, he probably needed the few cents he might save by not running the heater.

A sign to her right said they were ascending Willow Creek Pass. An occasional pickup or sport-utility vehicle passed from the other direction. No squirrels or other small animals scurried beside the road. No birds flew among the tall pines. A sign welcomed them to North Park. J.J. snorted under her breath. Welcome to three weeks of hell. Only colder. Much colder.

The pickup crested a hill, and North Park spread out below them, bathed in afternoon light. Mountains, intensely white with cobalt blue trees, surrounded the large, flat valley and threw blue shadows on the snow. Clouds sailed across the sky shading patches of the park's windswept snow. Groups of cattle dotted the white landscape. The disconnected blades of a windmill spun helplessly in the wind.

"Alexander expects you to sleep with me," Luke said in a conversational voice, turning the pickup off the main road.

The outrageous comment shocked J.J. from her silence. Jerking her head around, she stared at him. "What did you say?" A pickup passed, the occupants waving at Luke.

He waved back. "You heard me. When the three of us had dinner you absolutely refused to meet my terms. Then yesterday, you called me and agreed. It took me awhile to figure out why. Alexander thinks you've still got the hots for me, and he figured if you came up here, we'd sleep together and you'd get me out of your system."

"I have no intention of going anywhere near your bed, and if that's what you're planning, you can pull over right now, and I'll hitchhike back to Denver."

"He didn't apply pressure to get you to come?"

"Burton is a well-known, widely respected lawyer. One day he'll be appointed to the bench. He doesn't need me involving him in an unsavory divorce action." Burton had never even hinted at such a thing, but she had no intention of telling Luke the truth.

"I can't see Alexander worrying about the effect his wife's divorce would have on his career. I'd have guessed he'd demand to be judged on his record."

"I didn't say Burton was worried. I came because..." If coming up here set Burton's mind at ease, she'd do it. Burton's voiced concerns about her first marriage flooded her memory. She wondered if Luke was right. Had Burton erroneously labeled what he thought he'd sensed between Luke and J.J. as sexual tension? If so, he was wrong. The only thing between Luke Remington and J. J. O'Brien was embarrassment and a stupid marriage license. "Call it my wedding gift to him."

"An intriguing answer, which tells me exactly nothing."

"I'm here. Why, is none of your darned business."

Ahead a motley array of buildings hugged the landscape. Luke turned off the secondary road and drove beneath a huge log beam. Words, carved deep in the wood, spelled out Stirling Ranch. Esoteric ranch machinery littered the landscape around the cluster of buildings. J.J. glimpsed a long barn, two small houses and a trailer parked on cement blocks before Luke stopped in front of a two-story white-frame house.

"I probably ought to warn you, we weren't expecting you."

"I'm well aware of that." She didn't know much about Luke Remington, but one thing she was sure about. He'd been as surprised to see her at the gallery opening as she'd been to see him. "Just as I'm well aware your insistence on my coming here has nothing at all to do with me and everything to do with your childish pride."

Ignoring her words, Luke reached across and opened the passenger-side door. "You can get out here while I go take care of the horses."

Before J.J. could object, she found herself standing on a deep, covered porch, which ran the length of the front of the house. And what exactly was she supposed to say to the owners of the ranch when they answered the door? An image of the ranch gate with the owners' name flashed through her mind. Although tempting, "Mr. and Mrs. Stirling, I presume?" was hardly appropriate. Pressing the doorbell, she heard chimes peal inside.

Draperies in a nearby window parted slightly, then the door opened a couple of inches and a young, heavily made-up, female face peered out at J.J. "Yes?"

"I, uh, Luke told me to come here. He's doing something with the horses."

The woman twisted a dark brown ponytail around her

finger. "I didn't see Luke drive up." Her gaze searched behind J.J.

Looking for Luke? Or for some sign from the heavens that J.J. belonged on the porch? J.J. headed for a well-worn bench on the porch. "I can wait here."

"What?" The woman looked at J.J. as if she'd forgotten her. "It's cold out." She opened the door wider and stepped back.

J.J. took the opened door as invitation to enter. "Thank you. I'm sorry to intrude. I'm J. J. O'Brien." She had to give some explanation for appearing at the Stirlings' front door. Taking a deep breath, she plunged ahead. "Luke's wife."

"His wife!" The woman clutched her swollen belly. "Ethel never told me Luke was married."

"Ethel probably didn't know," J.J. said, too stunned to know what she was saying. A horrible suspicion turned her stomach as she looked at the slender, small-boned pregnant woman leaning against the closed front door. J.J. doubted the girl was seventeen years of age. A baby about to have a baby.

"Do I have to leave?" Brown eyes brimmed with fear and panic. "Luke said I could stay."

J.J. had thought when Luke warned her he hadn't expected her, he'd meant his trailer was dusty or had dirty clothes laying around. Instead he'd cruelly dumped her off to discover his pregnant girlfriend. He'd done it because she'd told him she intended to marry Burton after the divorce. Luke must have laughed himself silly when he heard she hadn't slept with Burton. Fury boiled over J.J. "You can stay."

The woman gave J.J. an uncertain smile. "I'm Birdie. You sure you don't mind me being here?"

"I'm sure." This child wasn't responsible for Luke's actions. An unexpected sadness replaced her anger. Whatever good memories J.J. had had of her short, foolish marriage were now vilely tainted. Her eyesight blurry, J.J. blindly turned on her heel to leave. She took one quick step before slamming into a solid mass.

"Whoa, O'Brien. Where's the fire? Where're you headed?"

Strong arms held her against a masculine bulk, her nose pressed into the cold, rough surface of a heavy coat. For a millisecond, J.J. felt safe and secure; then she remembered, and struggled to break free, her anger rekindled. "Back to Denver."

Luke let her move away, but he kept hold of her arms. "What's going on?"

"I can only guess what's going on now, but apparently quite a lot has gone on." J.J. jerked her head behind her.

"Hi, Birdie," Luke said. "I didn't see you standing there. Where's Ethel?"

"Her sister's husband up in Wyoming had a heart attack last night, and she went up this morning to help. I was starting dinner when this lady came in. I didn't know you was married," Birdie added plaintively.

"Damn. When's Ethel coming back? Why didn't she call me?"

"She tried. You'd left. She put a note on your desk."

Luke led J.J. down a short hall on the left to a room that obviously served as an office. Inside he shut the door. "We'll talk as soon as I've read Ethel's note." Removing his coat and tossing his wide-brimmed hat on one of the elk antlers hanging on the wall, he picked up a white sheet of paper from the surface of a scarred old dining-room table. "Sit." He pointed to an age-worn brown tweed sofa.

J.J. sat. Not because Luke told her to, but because she had a few things to say to Luke Remington before she left. While Luke read the letter, J.J. looked around the room. Piles of papers, magazines and books lay helter-skelter on almost every flat surface. A computer, telephone, small television, a stack of newspapers, basket of mail and a heavy mug filled with pencils and pens vied for space on the table. Windows on Luke's right faced ranch buildings backed by distant mountains.

Luke dropped the letter and walked around the table to lean a hip on the dark wood. He loomed over J.J. "Okay, O'Brien. I know the house isn't up to your sophisticated standards, but that's hardly cause to panic. I thought even you would last longer than five minutes."

"Panic!" She took a deep breath. Screeching at Luke might give him the impression she cared. Which she definitely did not. "I was not panicking. As soon as I saw Birdie I realized I didn't need to stay three weeks." Unable to stop herself, J.J. blurted out, "Luke, she's just a kid."

"Who, Birdie? Seventeen or eighteen, I guess. What's Birdie or how old she is have to do with you leaving?"

J.J. struggled to control her sagging jaw. "I married you without knowing enough about you," she said slowly, "but I thought I knew what kind of man you were." She hauled herself out of the chair, her muscles scarcely obeying her brain's command. "I was wrong."

Luke beat her to the office door. "Where do you think you're going? We have a deal, remember?" His outstretched arm held the door firmly shut.

"Not anymore." Luke Remington meant no more to her than she obviously had meant to him. J.J. didn't need to stay three weeks or even three minutes to know her short, intense infatuation for Luke had been a terrible mistake. Once Burton heard about Birdie, he'd agree. There was no way J.J. could love a deceitful, immoral tomcat. She wondered how many other women he'd slept with since their ill-considered marriage. "You fight this divorce and try to drag my name through the newspapers, and I'll destroy you. Our impulsive marriage was foolish and stupid, but your blackmail threats mean nothing now I know about Birdie."

"Know what about Birdie?"

"She's pregnant," J.J. hissed furiously.

"I know she's pregnant. I'm not blind." Halfway through the last word, Luke burst out laughing. "You think, me and Birdie? I'm practically old enough to be her father."

"Exactly."

"You've been spending too much time with people of low moral character, lawyer lady." Luke shifted, bracing himself with his hands pressed against the door on either side of J.J.. "Based on absolutely no evidence, you leaped to the crazy conclusion I'm the father of Birdie's baby. Why is that, O'Brien? Don't tell me you suffered a jealous fit at the thought of someone else sharing my bed."

J.J. didn't like his teasing conjecture any better than she liked his hard body crowding her against the door or the way his voice dropped seductively. She positively despised the sudden weakening in her knees. It wasn't her knees that were weak; it was her brain. "If you're not the father of the baby, why is Birdie so afraid I won't let her stay?"

Luke ran his hands up J.J.'s arms and across her shoulders. "Birdie's a timid little thing." One hand encircled her neck, his thumb resting against the pulse at the base of her throat. "She's been staying at Ethel's place and helping out around here. She's probably worried you'll change how things are run."

"I won't be here long enough to change anything."

"I never slept with Birdie, and you'll be staying three weeks." Luke captured her chin with his hand, spreading his fingers over her left cheek. "Disappointed?"

The heat from his hand penetrated her skin, spread throughout her body and then coalesced deep within her. J.J. tried to meld into the solid wood door at her back. A year had passed, everything had changed, yet nothing had changed. A simple touch and this thing between them, this insane infatuation, immediately burst into renewed life. She wanted nothing to do with it or with Luke. He'd asked her something. "Disappointed? To learn you didn't sleep with a child?"

Luke shook his head. "At losing your excuse for running away."

"I wasn't running away."

His fingers tightened on her face. "You're afraid. I can read it in your eyes. They're greener."

"The color of my eyes has nothing to do with fear. They change color according to what I'm wearing."

A slow, sexy smile curved Luke's lips. "You must be wearing green underwear. The rest of the stuff you're wearing wouldn't turn anything but someone's stomach."

He'd teased her before about her clothing. Her working clothes. Not her underwear. He'd never laughed at her underwear. Gleaming hazel eyes told her she wasn't the only one remembering. Her skin grew hot, her breathing shallow. It was happening again. Just like the first time. He was nothing but a bunch of parts, she told herself desperately. Squinty eyes, black eyelashes too long and thick for a man, missed whiskers in the slight cleft in his chin, a stubborn jawline, weather-tanned skin, dark brown hair flopping into his face... A mouth he'd used to kiss her stupid.

J.J. pressed her palms against the door behind her and stared at the faded black shirt inches from her beige coat. She'd come to prove her foolish infatuation for Luke Remington had been a momentary aberration. She would prove it. Determinedly she met his gaze. "We need a few ground rules if I'm going to stay here three weeks, and the first rule is—"

"The first rule is, I make the rules."

"The first rule is, you don't touch me."

"I like touching you." Luke slid his hand around to her nape, his fingers weaving upward through her short hair. "You used to like me touching you. Are you telling me that's changed, O'Brien?"

"We're getting divorced," she half whispered. "I'm going to marry someone else."

A dark slash of eyebrow rose quizzically. "Alexander? He's already having second thoughts. He knows he's the wrong man for you." Luke lowered his head.

His hands held her head captive, but she knew if she objected, he'd release her. This time. Better to let him kiss her. Once he had, he'd realize his kisses meant nothing to her. He wouldn't kiss her again.

His mouth closed firmly over hers. If she'd ever forgotten his kisses, her lips remembered. And parted at the memory. Luke edged closer, his body barely touching hers. Layers of clothing, including her down coat, separated them, yet J.J. felt every beat of his heart, every breath taken into his lungs.

Somehow he knew she was burning up, because, without lifting his mouth, he peeled her coat from her shoulders and arms. When the bulky garment caught between her hips and the door, Luke tugged her closer. Her breasts tingled and she leaned into him, locking her arms around his neck. They'd always fit perfectly together in spite of his six-inch height advantage. The coat slid slowly past her hips, falling to the floor with a whisper.

Luke's hands trailed slowly down the same path, stopping to cup the fullness of her hips. Then he gave her bottom a quick squeeze, lifted his head and took one step backward. "I've wanted to do that from the second I saw you the other night at the art gallery."

"Pinch me?" asked J.J. in a shaking voice. Cold air filled the space between them. She couldn't meet his eyes. In the V of his shirt his throat bore vestiges of a fading summer tan.

"Kiss you." Luke laughed softly. "That wasn't a pinch. I was making myself quit before I swept everything off the table and carried you over there to see if you were wearing green underwear.''

Heated longing swirled around J.J., then disappeared as if it were a fast-moving storm. He'd kissed her; she'd survived. "All right. You kissed me.''

"We kissed.''

"We kissed,'' she agreed, willing to concede one small point. "I'll even admit I liked kissing you, but that doesn't change anything. Marriage is about love, not kissing. Love doesn't mean doing irresponsible things like marrying a man days after you meet him. All we thought about was the physical pleasure we took from each other. I didn't touch you, kiss you, make, uh—''

"Make love,'' Luke said deliberately.

"All right, for lack of a better phrase. I didn't make love with you to please you. I did it for me. We only cared about satisfying our own selfish needs, getting the other into bed. People can't spend their whole marriage in bed.''

"We weren't always in bed.''

J.J.'s face flamed as Luke's words conjured up images of a woman as different from her normal, practical self as a woman could be. He didn't know the real J. J. O'Brien. With Luke she'd been a playful, inventive, hedonistic, sensual woman. An impulsive woman. A woman who'd tumbled into bed with a perfect stranger. She tried to explain. "We never talked about the future. I don't know anything about your family, where you grew up, your hopes, your dreams. You know nothing about who I am.''

"Hell, O'Brien, we lived together less than a week. Hardly time to relate our life histories.''

"A lot can be shared in a few days. All we shared was our bodies. I know nothing about the inner you.''

"I'd have told you anything you wanted to know,'' Luke said.

"I'm not blaming you. I never asked.'' Her face

flushed. "I didn't care. You looked at me, touched me, smiled at me, and all I could think about was the pleasure you gave me." She swallowed. "I'm more sorry and ashamed than I can ever say, but I didn't love you and I don't love you."

"Of course you didn't love me," Luke said impatiently. "Falling in love is for teenagers. Adults commit to each other, to their future. They work at building a life together. Love is their reward. We were physically attracted to each other, and I thought you were the kind of woman I wanted to share my life with. I thought we could build a future together. I was wrong. You don't want to share a man's life. You want him to tag along with yours."

Every one of J.J.'s brothers used to blame her when he didn't get his own way. Luke Remington was no different. "Burton and I will share each other's lives," she said stiffly. "We have a lot in common, think alike, have mutual interests, share the same tastes in movies, art, music. We believe in each other."

His mouth curved in disgust. "O'Brien, for a lawyer lady, you're about as dumb as dirt."

"You think anyone who disagrees with you is dumb. You wanted me to give up everything I'd worked for, that I'd dreamed of. For you. What were you going to give up for me?"

"I offered you half of everything I have, but that wasn't enough for you. You wanted everything your way." He shrugged. "If Burton doesn't mind being bossed around by you, it's no skin off my nose."

"For your information, I care about Burton, and he cares for me. I know about his past, know his hopes for the future. I know he needs me. And he's not having second thoughts."

Luke contemplated her for a long moment. "Burton won't make you happy because he believes the lies you spin, the person you invented, the costumes you wear."

"I do not—"

"The hell you don't. Shut up and let me finish."

J.J. shut up. For the moment.

"And because he believes, you'll never be able to let him know who you really are. Your life together would be a lie."

"He knows who—"

"I told you to keep your mouth shut." He pressed her head back against the door, his callused palm over her mouth. "How can he know? You don't know. You don't see it now, lawyer lady, but I'm doing you a favor." He smiled crookedly at the gobbling sounds she made. "I'm giving you three weeks to figure out who you are."

Something glittered in the depths of his eyes. "Maybe I'll use those three weeks to answer some questions of my own. I used to lay awake nights wondering why I thought you were a real woman, and wondering why the hell I married you. The answers to those questions could be interesting, don't you think, O'Brien?" He slid his palm from her mouth and ran a finger over her bottom lip.

J.J. suppressed an urge to wrap her lips around his finger. "I already know the answers. You wanted to sleep with me." The tip of her tongue brushed against the end of his finger.

"You think I couldn't have persuaded you into bed without a marriage license?"

"No. I mean, yes." How was she supposed to think when he distracted her by drawing circles around the small beauty mark at the corner of her mouth? "You couldn't have."

A knowing smile doubted her denial before fading away. "One other thing, O'Brien. You're not the only one who refrained from adulterous behavior. I haven't slept with another woman since our marriage." Moving her to one side, he opened the door. "I'll carry your stuff up to your room."

She wanted to ask him why he'd honored that particular wedding vow. Instead she objected to his dumping her on his employers. "I can't stay here." The Stirlings owned a ranch, not a hotel.

Luke grabbed her bags from near the front door. "I know it's not up to your usual standards, but you'll survive."

"It's not that. I assumed I'd stay at your place."

Luke headed up the narrow enclosed staircase. "Where do you think my place is?"

"Don't single ranch hands usually live in a trailer or something? It might be crowded, but we could manage."

"There's no way we could coexist in a trailer. I'd either end up wringing your neck, or..."

He didn't need to finish the sentence for J.J. to know what he meant. He needn't worry. It took two to tango and she had no intention of doing the tango or anything else with Luke Remington. "I can't inflict myself on perfect strangers," she protested to his back.

"Bathroom's there." Luke nodded to the right as he turned sharply into the room on the left at the top of the staircase. "We'll have to share it. My room's across the hall. This'll be your room."

J.J. halted in the doorway to the large bedroom. "Your room? You live with the Stirlings?"

"Zane Stirling died almost five years ago. I live by myself." Luke tossed J.J.'s luggage on the worn chenille bedspread, which might once have been white. "My wife lives in Denver."

"I am not a snob," J.J. told herself for the umpteenth time. She yanked the skin off a raw piece of chicken. Last year Luke had told her he was a cowboy. Anyone seeing his worn jeans, scarred boots and beat-up pickup truck would have guessed he didn't have two dimes to rub together. It wouldn't have killed him to have mentioned he managed the family ranch, fifty-five percent of

which he'd inherited from his uncle. Not that it mattered.
With a loud whack of the butcher knife J.J. severed the
chicken thigh from the leg. He could own a ranch the
size of Texas, and they'd still have nothing in common.

"What are you doing? Where's Birdie? What's this?"
Luke walked through the back door into the kitchen carrying the blackened skillet J.J. had set outside in the
snow.

She answered Luke's second question. "Birdie's over
at Ethel's house packing a bag. She's going to stay in
that small bedroom in the back until Ethel returns. The
room doesn't look as if it's used except for storage. I
cleared some space."

"Need a chaperone as well as a cook, O'Brien?"
Luke set the charred pan in the sink and leaned against
the cabinet, his hands braced on the countertop behind
him.

"Birdie is nervous about staying alone in an empty
house," J.J. said evenly.

"I finally reached Ethel on the phone." Luke watched
J.J. toss a couple of chicken pieces into a plastic bag of
flour, crumbs and spices. "She said her sister has gone
totally to pieces. Ethel could be up in Wyoming a week,
a month or more. I told her not to worry about us, we
could hold the fort here. Ethel didn't come right out and
say it, but I don't think we can expect much out of
Birdie." He crossed his booted feet at the ankles. "I
guess you'll be doing the cooking, O'Brien."

J.J. arranged the chicken on a baking sheet. She had
no trouble interpreting the amused speculation in Luke's
voice. In her Denver neighborhood a number of restau-
rants specialized in meals ready for patrons to pick up
on their way home from work, and Luke was remembering the deli meals, the take-out food, and the delivered pizzas they'd shared in Denver. J.J. knew he assumed she'd burnt the pan. She didn't think it worth

mentioning Birdie was the one who'd forgotten the oil heating in the pan.

She didn't feel challenged to prove she knew her way around a kitchen. On the other hand, she had to eat. "I can cook," she finally said. Her assurance failed to impress Luke.

A little over an hour later J.J. enjoyed the disbelief on Luke's face as he sat at one end of the dining-room table surveying the perfectly browned, oven-fried chicken, fluffy mashed potatoes, scalloped corn, applesauce muffins and tomato salad. Spreading a napkin over her lap, she bet herself he'd starve before admitting he'd been wrong about any of his assumptions about her.

"Where's Birdie?" Luke asked.

"I invited her to eat with us, but she preferred a tray in her room."

"Ethel usually fixes cream gravy with fried chicken."

J.J. met Luke's artless gaze across the corner of the table. "I'll bet her sister does, too. The sister whose husband is in the hospital with a coronary attack."

"Don't tell me you're a health food nut. I like meat on the table."

Maybe he'd like it in his lap. A model of restraint, she handed Luke the bowl of salad. "You'll get it. In moderation. My dad and Kenny are doctors, my mother's a nurse, and Logan's in med school. I know more than I want about clogged arteries."

Luke piled his plate with food. "Kenny and Logan?"

"Two of my brothers."

"There's more?"

"Two more. Blaine teaches biology back in Iowa, and Brendan is at the university majoring in bio-chem."

"Does your family know you're married?"

J.J. concentrated on removing chicken meat from the bone. "Mom and Dad have been married almost thirty-seven years. They believe in bringing potential mates home for inspection, long engagements and big church weddings. Over three hundred people were invited to Kenny and Casey's wedding."

"They don't know." When J.J. didn't respond, he asked, "Did you take Alexander home with you at Christmas to meet the family?"

"Of course not. He and his daughter, Carrie, spent Christmas with Burton's first wife's parents in Boulder. Burton's a widower." She avoided meeting Luke's eyes.

The anniversary clock in the living room chimed the hour. As the last chime faded away, Luke asked grimly, "When *did* you introduce him to your parents as your future husband?"

CHAPTER THREE

"WHAT makes you think I introduced Burton to anyone as my future husband?" The minute the question left her mouth J.J. knew it incriminated her. She should have given Luke an immediate denial. "Thanksgiving," she muttered into her potatoes. "Carrie went on a ski trip with friends, and Burton flew back to Iowa with me for the long weekend. But we didn't say anything about getting married." Not that her family hadn't made a few guesses, which she'd cowardly chosen to ignore.

"Why not?"

J.J. wished Luke would quit grilling her and eat his dinner. Might as well wish she could wiggle her nose and transport her body back to her Denver town house. To a time before she'd met Luke Remington. His unrelenting silence finally goaded her into answering. "It's awkward, okay? Mom saved her wedding dress for me to wear at my wedding. She won't understand Burton and I having a modest ceremony in front of a judge."

"You'll have to tell her sometime."

"There's no rush." She doggedly ate her dinner. "I have to get divorced first, remember?"

"I'm not likely to forget."

"To this day I can't believe I actually married a total stranger. Nobody held a gun to my head, I was perfectly sober, there's no mental illness in my family... What was I thinking?"

"The same thing I was thinking?"

J.J. gave him a murderous look. "Why didn't we just sleep together? We didn't have to get married to have sex."

"You weren't into casual sex," Luke said evenly, "and I wanted you."

"Yeah, right." J.J. reduced her muffin to crumbs. "It's my stupid mouth with its stupid fat bottom lip. If I've had one man, I've had a dozen, tell me how they adore my sexy pout. It's enough to make a woman gag." She gazed skyward. "And thanks, Nika, for the dumb beauty mark."

"Nika?"

"An ancestor of my mom's from way back. Supposedly a member of the Russian aristocracy. My mom has a picture of her." J.J. laughed shortly. "My dad says we're imperfectly blended blender kids. English, Irish, German, Finnish, Russian, Slavic, French and American Indian genes all tossed into the blender, only somebody turned off the machine before we homogenized. Not only do we all look totally different, we're all chunks of this or that. Lucky me got the pouty bottom lip and beauty mark so I look like some kind of bimbo sexpot. Do you have any idea how hard it is to convince a male client I have an IQ over ten when I look like this?"

"I like your mouth."

"Of course you do. Men are so shallow. Never mind, my brothers insist the color of my hair is mousy brown, my colorless face looks like an anemic square, my eyes are faded aqua and my eyebrows are practically nonexistent. All you men see is the mouth and the beauty mark."

"You should be grateful. If I hadn't seen that provocative little beauty spot, I'd have let the horse run over you."

J.J. pointed her fork at him. "It's not funny...it's a curse. Because of this darned face, I've had to work harder and longer than any ten men. Men wear a shirt the color of their eyes, and people admire the shirt. I wear a pretty dress and some jerk pats my behind, or I'm accused of using my sex as some kind of weapon.

When a man wins a case, people praise his abilities. If I win, there's always someone who says I flirted with the male jury members. Newspapers discuss a man's legal arguments—they talk about my hair. You don't know what it's like to spend your entire life fighting to prove yourself.''

"Everybody grows up proving himself." Luke spread butter on a muffin. "Take me. I'm an army brat. I started out fighting kids whose dads were enlisted. I had to prove I wasn't soft because my dad was an officer. The older I got, the more trouble I got into. It wasn't enough to prove I wasn't a goody-two-shoes, I had to lead the pack of troublemakers. Later, I had to prove I was as tough as my dad even though I refused to follow in his footsteps and go to West Point.''

"And now you're proving how tough you are by forcing me to bend to your will for three weeks. Daddy must be proud.''

"Bend to my will?" Luke snorted. "Tell another one, O'Brien. We both know you're not here because I threatened to fight the divorce if you didn't come." He leaned back in his chair. "One of these days I'll figure out exactly why you did come.''

"Not because I want us to reconcile.''

"Reconcile!" The shock on Luke's face was hardly flattering to J.J. "I sure as hell hope not. I've spent the past year thanking my lucky stars you gave me my walking papers.''

"Thanking your..." Speech temporarily failed her. "Then why didn't you immediately agree to our obtaining a divorce?" J.J. asked in exasperation.

"I would have if you'd written me a letter asking for one. Unfortunately I saw you." Memories blazed deep in his eyes. "Crowded as the art gallery was, I spotted you the instant I walked through the door. While I watched you, this damned movie kept fast-forwarding through my head. Starring you and me in your apartment."

"Town house," J.J. said automatically, fighting in vain to keep those same images out of her head.

"I kept seeing your sheets. A pale pink, the color of your skin."

"Shell pink." She told herself the dry climate caused any electricity in the air.

"I thought I'd managed to forget what you keep hidden under those ugly businessmen suits of yours, but seeing you again—" his voice thickened "—I wanted you. As much as before."

J.J.'s heart skipped a beat. Luke still wanted her. The knowledge pleased her, in itself a terrifying revelation. She didn't want him to want her. She didn't want to want him. Infatuation flew in the face of good sense and reason, and she'd always been a sensible, reasonable person. Only Luke had had the power to transform her into an impulsive stranger. She couldn't let him beguile her again. "Is that why you insisted I come? To satisfy your hormonal urges once more?"

"Hell no." Shock turned to horror on his face. "Just the opposite. I figure three weeks of you whining and complaining and demonstrating how totally unfit you are to live here will be all I need to erase you and your pale blue underwear from my head forever. If and when I marry again, my wife won't be as soft as the skin under that silk underwear of yours. And she won't be pseudotough, pretending she's as good as any man. She'll be a woman, a real woman," he emphasized, "soft where a woman's supposed to be soft and strong where a woman's supposed to be strong. The kind of woman you don't know anything about."

"I know all about the kind of woman you want. One who hops into bed when you snap your fingers and hops out to cook your breakfast or wash your socks when you snap your fingers again."

Luke snapped his fingers, his gaze locked on J.J. She glared back, not moving a muscle. "Yup," he said, "you're definitely not the kind of woman I want for my wife."

J.J. scowled at the phone sitting on the office table desk. When she'd told Burton about the ranch, he'd said she ought to have realized Luke had too much self-possession to be a mere employee. A diploma on the wall caught her eye. Luke had graduated from Colorado State University. Another little tidbit he'd neglected to mention.

She looked around the room, curling her lip at the elk antlers. From the little she'd seen of the ranch house, it seemed to be furnished in a mixture of Oregon Trail castoffs and garage sale leavings. Definitely not to her taste. At least the unknown Ethel, who'd turned out to be Luke's housekeeper, kept the place spotlessly clean.

"Mrs. Remington?"

J.J. looked up. Birdie hovered in the doorway to the hall leading to the kitchen, nervously twisting around her finger a small section of the hair hanging lank around her shoulders. J.J. gave the young woman a reassuring smile. "Call me J.J."

A timid smile flickered across Birdie's thin lips. "J.J.'s a funny name for a woman."

J.J. wrinkled her nose. "My mother named me Jacqueline June and said no one was to call me Jackie. Then my brother Logan came along, and he had trouble saying Jacqueline so my name came out sounding like J.J. Soon everyone called me J.J."

"Did your ma get mad?"

J.J. rolled her eyes. "My brothers can charm my mother in or out of anything they want."

"Ad's like that with Ma."

"Aid?"

Birdie gathered the hem of her maternity top in a

bunch and wrapped it around one hand. "My husband, Adrian. With Ethel gone..." Her face paled. "I got scared, not knowing what to do. She left her sister's number, and I called her from her place. She said I gotta tell Luke so he'll know it's important Ad don't know I'm here. I don't want to tell Luke, he's a man, but Ethel said I gotta think of the baby." She twisted the fabric tighter around her fist. "I thought maybe, you being a woman, you'd tell Luke for me."

"Tell Luke what?" Prior experience warned J.J. she wouldn't like Birdie's answer. Birdie walked into the light cast by the lamp on the table. Her bruised face, devoid of makeup, confirmed J.J.'s suspicions. Faded blue circles, like fingerprints, ran down the sides of Birdie's neck. J.J. took a deep breath and slowly exhaled. Shocked exclamations wouldn't help Birdie. "Husbands have no right to hit their wives," she said quietly.

"Ad didn't mean to hurt me. It was my fault, nagging him about his drinking. He was real sorry the next day. I wouldn't of left just cuz of this," she added defensively, "no matter what Ethel said when she saw me in the grocery store 'bout how I shouldn't let him get away with hitting me."

"I expect your injuries upset Ethel."

"That's cuz she doesn't understand about Ad. Things've always been hard for him. His pa was dirt poor and no one ever gave him nothing. I shouldn't nag on him for spending a few dollars on beer. He'll give me money when the baby comes. I shouldn't have been bothering him with it now. It was my fault, I know that, but—" she cradled her stomach "—I couldn't let him hurt the baby. So I came to Ethel like she said I should."

"Hurt the baby?" J.J. asked, her facial muscles rigidly maintaining a composed expression.

"I shoulda known he'd had a bad day, that it was a bad time to be asking for money for a crib and such, but he shouldn't blame the baby for that. When he throwed me against the wall and used his belt on me, he could of hurt the baby.''

J.J. squeezed her eyes closed until she felt she could control her voice. ''A mother wants to protect her unborn child.''

''Ad said I'd be sorry if I ever left him, but I snuck out. Just for now. He'll be okay after the baby comes. He'll love the baby.'' Her hand crept up to the bruise on her cheek. ''Ethel said she'd keep Ad away from me, but she's gone, and I'm scared Ad will find me and drag me back by my hair. He done that once when I went home to Ma, and Pa said a husband and wife should settle stuff between themselves. Ethel said to tell Luke so Ad won't hurt me or my baby. Luke won't let Ad make me go home, will he?''

''Luke won't let your husband hurt you or force you to go home.'' Funny how J.J. knew so little about Luke, but she knew that. ''You and the baby are safe here.'' Now wasn't the time for suggestions, all of which she knew Birdie would reject. Women like Birdie always did.

After Birdie left, J.J. swiveled Luke's office chair around and stared out the uncurtained window into the black starless night. Not for the first time she wondered how any woman could accept violence as normal in a marriage. She closed her eyes, hearing in her head Birdie's justification for her husband's behavior. As if anything excused the bruises on Birdie.

''You okay?''

The quiet question came from the doorway across the room from where Birdie had exited. J.J. didn't turn. ''Why wouldn't I be?'' She heard Luke's footsteps cross the floor. The door to the kitchen hallway closed with a click.

''I was on my way in here when I heard Birdie. I didn't think she'd welcome an audience.''

"So you eavesdropped." J.J. had to lash out at someone. "You cowboys are so darned—damned—" she spit out the swear word "—macho and tough, you probably think yanking a wife around by her hair is a sign of affection."

"Damn it, O'Brien..." With a hard thrust, Luke swung his office chair around so J.J. faced him.

Squeezing the chair's padded arms, J.J. stared blindly past him. "Don't swear at me."

Luke gently touched her cheek. "O'Brien, don't." He extracted a white handkerchief from a back pocket and handed it to her. "Blow."

J.J. blew. "Quit bossing me around." She blew again. "I think I'm allergic to cow dust or something."

"Ad Parker's not a cowboy." Luke circled behind the chair and kneaded her shoulders and the top of her spine. "Ethel said the two were having problems. I didn't know Ad knocked Birdie around." He paused. "It's an open secret Dan Clayton, Birdie's dad, hits her mom now and then. Ev Bailey, the sheriff, has been trying to get Dee to press charges, but she refuses. Says Dan still has a lot of anger from being in Vietnam. You'd think Birdie would have learned something from them."

J.J. sniffled. "I'm sure she did. When you see your dad beat up your mom, you think that's how married life is supposed to be. I've had women tell me, 'That's just his way.'" She swiped at her nose with Luke's wadded-up hanky. "It's the wrong way." She sniffled again. "I'm sorry I hollered at you. It's not your fault Birdie's husband abuses her. Abused wives are usually so embarrassed by it, many believing they deserve what they get, they keep the abuse secret. Birdie wouldn't have told me if she wasn't worried about the baby."

Luke dug into her back with his thumbs. "You're right about one thing," he said abruptly. "We don't know much about each other." He hesitated. "Dinner tonight was delicious."

The compliment came as a surprise. J.J. leaned back against the chair and looked up. "Why did you assume I couldn't cook?"

Luke stopped massaging. "I have two images of you," he said slowly, his eyes holding hers. "You in one of those sexless bags you wear to work—a poster for the career woman out to emasculate men. The other is you in that pale cream-colored night thing—" his fingers tightened "—that drove me wild." He gave her a lopsided grin. "I never picture you in an apron."

Luke was right. His eyes weren't like marbles. Agate was cold. Luke's eyes warmed her all the way through to her spine. J.J. thought of drowsy summer days when silt floated on ponds in mysterious, swirling patterns of gray and brown and blue. She swallowed hard. "Mom and Dad expected us kids to share the load around the house. We can all cook. Not gourmet. Don't expect gourmet. Just basic stuff. Meat loaf is my specialty." She couldn't stop the senseless words spilling from her mouth. Her neck ached from looking up.

Luke slid around the chair and sat on the edge of the desk table. With one easy move, he pulled J.J. to her feet. "I love meat loaf," he murmured, his hands loosely encircling her waist.

She stood between his hard thighs. There was no place to put her hands except on his upper arms. She clutched the hanky and concentrated on Luke's chin. A year had passed, yet her tongue retained memories of the rasping feel of his whiskers and the taste of his cleft. "Salty." The muttered word clicked her brain back on. "My meat loaf," she said quickly. "It's not too salty. I'm known for my pot roast, too."

Luke pulled her closer, his eyes surveying her face. "I can hardly wait."

"Why are you looking at me like that?"

"I'm looking for a dry spot to kiss."

''That's not why I'm here, remember? You don't want to kiss me,'' J.J. said. ''You want—''

''You.'' His hands slid down to slowly massage her bottom.

''We're supposed to be getting a divorce, not getting into bed.'' Which one of them was she reminding?

''Maybe we're going about this divorce thing all wrong.''

''We are.'' J.J. tried for firmness. ''Quit trying to kiss me. And move your hands.''

''I am moving them.''

''I mean away from my...away from me.''

''What is it about you, O'Brien? What kind of black magic do you cook up? You're as addictive as drugs.''

When she'd told him to move his hands, she hadn't meant to her rib cage. It took no imagination to remember the feel of his fingers on her naked skin. Her head told her they were wrong for each other. Her body sang an entirely different tune. She refused to listen. ''Physical attraction. That's all. And it's not enough. You know it's not enough. It's like junk food. I need a balanced, wholesome diet.''

Luke's gaze roamed up and down J.J. His hands held her prisoner. ''When I was ten, I complained about my mother's cooking, said I preferred hot dogs. She told me if I liked hot dogs so much, I could eat them from then on. No matter what the family ate, she fixed me hot dogs. The first few days I ate those hot dogs with gusto. They didn't taste quite so good when she cooked my favorite meals for the others. By the end of the first week, it took all I had to convince Mom I still preferred hot dogs to her cooking. I conceded her the battle midway through the second week. For years afterward I couldn't so much as look at a hot dog.''

''A charming anecdote.'' Was he aware his thumb had wandered up to casually encircle her nipple? She grabbed his hand to stop him and somehow succeeded in pressing his palm over her breast. J.J. didn't think all the calluses in the world could keep Luke from noticing the way her nipple hardened at his touch. "But what it's got to do with anything, I can't imagine."

"Substitute you for hot dogs."

"That's even more charming." Sarcasm somehow lost its punch when accompanied by quickened breathing. She'd spent years studying law and had never learned anything useful, such as how to make slow, sexy smiles illegal.

"I've been thinking." He slid a button through the top buttonhole of her blouse. "Maybe we should sleep together and get it out of our systems. It shouldn't take long. Not only do we have nothing else in common, but you hog the covers."

"I do not." No one would guess she was a lawyer known for her cross-examination skills.

He unbuttoned a second button. "By the end of three weeks we'll be so bored with each other—" a third button, then a fourth slipped free "—if you were to stand in front of me stark naked doing the hula—" Luke trailed his hands up to J.J.'s collarbone, using his thumbs to slide open her blouse "—you wouldn't cause even a rising blip in my blood pressure." Gripping her shoulders with his hands, he pulled her close, his mouth level with the pulse beating at the base of her throat.

His lips seared her flesh, reducing her objections, if she could think of any, to ashes. She parted her mouth at his urging and told herself his reasoning was sound. She'd always preached moderation in all things. An overdose of anything could be deadly. An overdose of Luke Remington would cure the juvenile infatuation raging through her blood.

She wanted to sleep with him. They were married. Sleeping together for three little weeks wouldn't hurt. They could still get divorced. She could still marry

Burton. Burton. A sudden chill invaded her bones, and J.J. lifted her mouth from Luke's.

"No, don't." She pulled his hands away from her. "You're messing up my mind. Making the ridiculous sound sensible. What you're suggesting wouldn't be smart. I don't understand why you excite my hormones the way you do," she added with painful honesty, "but I intend to fight it. My way." Clutching the front of her blouse together she headed for the office door with as much dignity as she could muster.

"Okay, we'll play it your way. For now."

She forced herself to turn and face him. His eyes told her he wanted her; his patient smile said he knew she wanted him and he was willing to wait. J.J. wanted to hurl herself across the room and back into his arms. She said, "We'll play it my way for the next three weeks and forever."

Luke stood, arrogantly widening his smile. He practically swaggered to the door where J.J. stood, her fingernails digging into the wooden molding. Sliding a finger beneath the lace edging her seafoam-colored silk bra, he said in a low, throaty growl, "I'll say one thing, O'Brien, you still have excellent taste in underwear." His knuckle inflamed her skin. "Anytime you want to join me in bed—my door is always open to my wife."

J.J. fled to her bedroom.

Sleep refused to come. She looked around the strange room. Luke's uncle's room, Luke had said when she'd asked. The utilitarian room contained an old, chipped white iron bed and a single, unadorned dresser of oak. Beside the bed a small chest of drawers painted a hideous shade of brown served as a night table. Old-fashioned light sconces hung above the bed. She twisted her head to read the signature on the Western print above the bed. C. M. Russell.

In Denver, the sounds outside her town house—traffic, music, car doors slamming, even barking dogs—sang muted songs that lulled J.J. to sleep. Here, the unfamiliar creaks and groans of the old house made her twitch restlessly beneath the blankets.

The silver-framed photograph sitting on the bedside chest drew her eye. Burton and Carrie posed on the steps of the state capitol building in Denver. Their smiles looked forced. Loneliness shadowed their faces. Burton's gaze—a sad, faintly resigned one—looked directly at J.J.

Burton's voiced concerns about J.J. loving Luke echoed around the room. She shook her head at the photo. Luke Remington's presence across the hall had nothing to do with her insomnia. No compassionate person would be able to sleep after hearing Birdie's sad tale. Except the self-assured mouth J.J. saw when she closed her eyes wasn't Birdie's. The rising wind howled around corners and whistled under the eaves. Foretelling a change in the weather. Or laughing heartily at J.J.

Light filtered through the threadbare curtains to dimly light the bedroom. J.J. frowned at the clock on the bedside chest. At this hour there ought to be more light. Her bare feet cringed as they hit the freezing wood floor. She went to the window and pulled aside a curtain. A world of white greeted her. The falling snow not only cut out the sunlight, but the other ranch buildings had disappeared from view making the ranch house an island, isolated from the rest of the world. Exploring the ranch would have to wait for better weather.

J.J. headed back to bed. Knuckles rapped loudly on the bedroom door. Pulling the covers up under her chin, she asked Luke what he wanted.

"Breakfast," he said, opening her door and poking his head in. "You're the cook, remember?"

"I'll cook when I get up. It's snowing too hard to do anything now. Go back to bed."

Luke moved into the room. "This isn't the city where

everyone goes to work late on snowy days. Cows and horses eat 365 days a year."

"Good for them." J.J. turned her back to him. "Maybe they'll let you share their breakfast."

"C'mon, cookie. Let's go."

Feeling his hand touch the covers and guessing his intent, J.J. tightly gripped her blankets, prepared to fight for them. With lightning speed, Luke swept the covers from her bed. J.J., hanging on for dear life, followed her flying blankets to the floor. She landed facedown in a sprawl on the heap of heavy blankets. "Darn you, Luke Remington," she spat, coming up for air. "I could have broken something."

"You should have let go," he said in a reasonable voice.

"Maybe I didn't want to let go." She rolled over to glare up at him. "Don't think you can bully me. If I want, I'll sleep here on the floor until I'm good and ready to get up."

"Fine with me." He stood over her, his booted feet on either side of her, his hands resting easily on his hips.

The warm intensity in Luke's eyes as he looked down vanquished the legions of goose bumps marching over J.J.'s skin. She followed his gaze. Her precipitous descent from bed had twisted the hem of her lilac silk ankle-length negligee around her upper thighs and dislodged the thin straps of the gown's bodice. A rosy nipple, hardened by the room's chill air, peeped above creamy lace.

Mortified, J.J. yanked up the top of the gown and struggled to sit up and tug down the gown's hem. Not only did the tight proximity of Luke's boots make the task difficult, but the dumb ox stood on her expensive silk negligee. "Do you think you could possibly move?" she asked through gritted teeth.

"I could, but I'm enjoying the scenery."

J.J. had four brothers. If they'd taught her one thing,

it was that it took brains and audacity to defeat brute strength. In a quick series of lithe moves, J.J. wiggled out of the negligee. Gaining her freedom, she marched in triumphant naked splendor to the closet and grabbed her down-filled bathrobe. Without breaking stride, she flung the robe over her shoulders and stomped on bare feet to the bathroom. Leaving Luke standing stunned on the abandoned silk gown.

The snow had stopped falling, allowing the sun to break through the clouds. The cold air sparkled in the sunshine, and every inch of the ranch yard glittered with tiny white diamonds. J.J. followed Luke's path to the barn through drifts above her knees, carefully placing her feet where he'd stepped. She didn't even want to know what the temperature was. Fortunately she hadn't argued when Luke insisted she bring her ski pants, and she'd taken him up on his loan of his uncle's old sheepskin jacket. Worn over a knit shirt and two sweaters, the jacket hung to her knees and covered her gloved hands. A fuzzy-lined cap with ear flaps completed her less-than-fashionable outfit. Cows didn't have much fashion sense, and J.J. didn't expect to meet anyone else.

She didn't particularly want to meet Luke. With the exception of a few snickers at the breakfast table, which she'd quelled by threatening him with the pancake turner, he hadn't commented on her early-morning strip-tease. Maybe he couldn't believe what he'd seen. J.J. couldn't believe what she'd done, but at that particular moment, standing up to Luke had seemed of utmost importance. From her brothers she'd learned all too well the lesson that backing down even once meant exposing a weak spot others were quick to take advantage of.

Now she wished she hadn't reacted instinctively, but had thought the situation through. She should have tried for tears or bitterly complained. Either would have disgusted Luke. Maybe she wouldn't have had to stay here three weeks. So what if he thought her a weak namby-pamby? His opinion didn't matter. All that mattered was dissolving their marriage.

The hand on J.J.'s shoulder flinging her around took her by total surprise. Only the heavy-handed grip kept her from sprawling headlong in the snow. From the look on the face of the man who'd waylaid her, she wasn't the only one surprised.

"Who the hell are you?" he demanded.

Antagonized by his rudeness, J.J. deliberately plucked his hand from her shoulder and stepped away before saying, in an overly polite voice, "I don't believe I caught your name, either." Luke needed to teach his cowhands a few manners.

The man stuck his thumbs into the back pockets of his dirty jeans, and rocked back on his heels, his gaze scrutinizing every inch of J.J.'s exposed face. He might have been handsome were it not for pockmarked skin and flat, black eyes. J.J. guessed he was about her age. "Well, well, ol Luke's gone and found hisself a play-mate," he said in an insolent voice. "If the rest of you's anything like your sweet mouth, you're wasted on him." A slight breeze stirred long greasy black hair hanging below a filthy, battered cowboy hat. "What say you and me head into town and share a beer, sweet mouth?"

Some men ought to be put down like rabid dogs. "No, thank you," J.J. said civilly. "I have other plans." She turned to continue on to the barn.

The man roughly grabbed her arm, swinging her around. "It ain't polite, sweet mouth, to walk away when a man's talking."

J.J. stifled a sigh. Great. A caveman whose brain ran on testosterone. He'd view heated opposition as a challenge to prove his manhood. "You invited me for a beer," she said evenly. "I politely declined. I don't believe there's anything more to discuss."

"Now, sweet mouth—" his hand tightened on her

arm "—don't be in such a hurry to run off." He gave her a cocksure smile. "I ain't through talking with you." He pulled her closer. "How 'bout a kiss?"

There were times J.J. regretted she didn't have the kind of hands one registered as lethal weapons. She longed to smack this creep right in the middle of his leering face. Instead she said, "I hope you've had your shots. The doctor said I'm still extremely infectious. I didn't think that kind of disease could be transmitted just by a kiss, but..." She shrugged.

He took one step back before blustering, "Maybe I like living dangerously."

"I hope so, Parker, because when you put your filthy hands on my wife, you're living extremely dangerously." The sharp edge in Luke's voice could have cut stone.

J.J. swiveled. Luke stood in the huge, open barn doorway. An enormous light brown horse peered curiously over his shoulder.

"Hey—" the cowhand backed away from J.J., his hands up in a caricature of surrender "—she never told me she belonged to you."

"I don't belong to anyone," J.J. said in annoyance, moving away from the cowhand.

Both men ignored her. "What do you want, Parker?"

"My wife. I heard she was hanging around here. Is she?"

"I don't keep track of other men's wives." Luke's already hard stare fossilized. "But I take good care of my own."

"It ain't my fault she didn't tell me who she is," the man whined. "I wouldn't mess with your wife."

"I'm glad to hear that, Parker, because I'm real particular about who touches her. That being so, you'll understand why I don't want you coming around here bothering her again."

"Whatever you say, man. Ain't no woman worth hassling over."

Luke moved to J.J.'s side, and they watched the man get in his truck. The engine revved, the wheels spun momentarily in the snow, and then the truck bounced out of the ranch yard and through the gate. The minute the truck disappeared down the road, J.J. put aside her resentment to ask the question she'd been holding back since Luke appeared. "Is he Birdie's husband?" At Luke's grunted assent, she said, "No wonder Birdie left him."

She shuddered extravagantly. "What a cretin. Why did he think Birdie might be here? Do you think he believed you?" J.J. frowned. "I hope he doesn't figure out you didn't exactly deny she was here. He probably won't. His IQ must be about the same as his shoe size." It occurred to her she was carrying on this conversation single-handedly. "Why don't you say something?"

"Just what do you want me to say, O'Brien?"

Luke's caustic tone rekindled her resentment. "Not a thing. I wouldn't want you to strain yourself. Polite conversation is obviously beyond your limited capabilities. This valley must breed Neanderthal throwbacks."

"You want conversation? Okay, how's this for conversation." The horse threw up his head and snorted uneasily at Luke's snarling voice. "Why the hell didn't you open your mouth and say the three little words that would have kept Parker from bothering you? Here." Luke thrust leather reins at her.

J.J. automatically took them. "What three little words?" she hollered as Luke disappeared into the barn. "Don't touch me? You disgust me? I want to throw up? Oh, sorry," she said sarcastically, "that's more than three words."

The crunching of snow under an enormous hoof alerted her to a fact she'd previously neglected to absorb. The reins Luke had tossed at her were attached to the giant horse. A horse that grew in size as he walked toward J.J. "Good horse," she said nervously, stepping backward. "Listen, Trigger, or whatever your name is, quit following me." The horse pointed his ears toward J.J. and kept pace with her backward retreat. J.J. opened her mouth to call Luke, then snapped it shut. Luke coming to her rescue twice in one day would be insupportable.

The immense animal plodded after her, blotting out the sun. "Stop, horse. Whoa." The horse lowered his white-striped head and butted J.J. in the stomach. She backpedaled faster. The horse butted her again, then turned his head slightly to look at her. The huge eye, its pupil an ominous narrow horizontal slit, told J.J. this horse didn't like her. She speeded up, heading backward toward the wooden corral, planning to climb up out of the monster's reach.

Her eyes locked on the horse, J.J. failed to see the small bale of hay mounded with snow. The bale caught her behind her knees and she pitched backward into the snow, her legs sticking up in the air. The horse walked around the bale, lowered his head and opened an enormous mouth filled with huge, menacing teeth. From his throat came the most diabolical sound J.J. had ever heard.

CHAPTER FOUR

LUKE took one look at J.J.'s predicament and broke out laughing. Grabbing the reins from her, he shoved the horse to one side and reached out to help J.J. up.

Ignoring his hand, she struggled to her feet and beat snow off her clothes. Snow inside her coat collar fell down the back of her neck, freezing her skin. It did nothing to cool her temper. "If I'd come here before I let you brainwash me into marrying you, I would have known what a sadistic brute you were. Siccing a vicious animal like that on me." She took off her hat and smacked it against her knee to remove the snow.

"I'm sorry." Luke choked out the words between gusts of laughter. "It never occurred to me you'd be afraid of horses."

"I'm not afraid of horses," J.J. said, backing away as she realized a second horse, a twin of the first, trailed Luke. "That's not a horse, it's an elephant. He tried to bite me."

"Not Johnny. He was trying to tell you he wanted a treat. He's as gentle as a newborn lamb." Luke rubbed the horse's long face. "You haven't forgotten your old friend Zane, have you, fella? Did you smell him on the coat or were you sniffing for the carrots he brought you?" The horse gave a low nicker and nibbled Luke's shoulder. The second horse moved up and stuck his nose between them. "Quit begging, you two. Work first, then your treat." He backed the two horses to a low, flat sled and quickly harnessed them to it. Holding the horses easily in check, he said to J.J., "Hop on."

Encumbered with heavy clothing, J.J. could hardly

60

hop, but she managed to scramble onto the sled. A huge tractor pulling an empty trailer clattered out the other side of the yard.

"Why didn't you let go of the reins?" Luke asked.

The sled took off with a lurch. J.J. clung to the four-foot-high wooden crossbars in front. "I worried he'd run away."

Luke gave her an odd look. "You're something else, O'Brien."

"I'm a lawyer, not a cow person," she said hotly. "The closest I've ever been to a horse is that time at the stock show when we met. Don't sneer at me because you think that behemoth of yours made me a trifle nervous."

"I wasn't sneering. I'm impressed you hung on. Most women who've never been around Belgian draft horses would have been terrified by Johnny's rooting around in their clothing while they were wearing it. They would have fled without giving one thought as to whether or not the horse took off."

"I was not terrified," J.J. said indignantly, "and that's a sexist remark. Women are no more or less cowardly or brave than men." Her earlier grievance still rankled. "And we don't stand around waiting for men to rescue us from morons like Birdie's husband. I could have handled him."

The good humor on Luke's face evaporated. "We didn't finish that discussion, did we?" He halted the horses beside a stack of hay bales. Wrapping the reins around an upright board on the sled, he picked up a wicked-looking tool and began hooking bales and stacking them on the other end of the sled.

"What's to discuss? The three little words I'm supposed to have used against him as some sort of magic incantation?"

"We can start with that." Luke had been stacking the

bales four high and now he slammed a bale down next
to J.J.

No wonder he had such nice shoulders, J.J. thought
before mentally slapping herself. Admiring Luke's physique is what got her into trouble in the first place.
"Well? What three words?"

"You know damned good and well what three
words." He tossed the last bale into place and rammed
the metal implement into the top bale. "'I'm Luke's
wife.' If you'd said them, Parker would have left you
alone."

"Oh, those three words." J.J. stared at the broad
equine rumps moving placidly ahead of them. Not once
in over a year of marriage had she said those words. At
least, not out loud. The harness jingled and the sled's
runners whistled against the snow. The horses puffed
vapor from their nostrils, and their huge feet sent up
clouds of snow with each step. The hay bales behind J.J.
smelled like late-summer Iowa harvests. She changed the
subject. "Why don't you use the tractor?"

"Jeff and Dale are using it to pick up those big hay
rolls from the stacks we passed yesterday. They'll feed
the cows down in the lower creek pasture and over in
the south pasture." Luke stopped the horses, secured the
reins and jumped down to open a gate. Leaving it ajar,
he guided the horses through, then closed the gate behind them. Swinging back up on the sled, he said, "Zane
insisted tractor noise is too stressful for the heifers. I
thought he just liked to drive the team, and after he died,
I considered retiring Hondo and Johnny, but..." He
shrugged.

"I'm sure he's pleased you've kept up the tradition."

Luke grinned. "More'n likely he'd say, 'Criminy,
Sarge, you getting sentimental on me?'"

J.J. heard the deep affection for his uncle in Luke's
voice, and she started to ask him about Zane Stirling and
why he called Luke "Sarge," but the cows trotting from

every nook and cranny toward the sled captured her complete attention. The cattle mooed loudly, and a couple broke into a run. "Uh, Luke, we're about to be besieged."

"They're hungry." Luke wrapped the reins loosely around the post on the sled. "Okay, boys, steady now." Grabbing the hook, he sliced the wire around the bales and threw the hay to the ground. The horses plodded steadily in an elongated circuit of the pasture, totally ignoring the cows.

J.J. had more trouble ignoring the cows as they snatched at the hay on the sled. She hoped they could discriminate between her and their food.

At the far end of the pasture, the team stopped. Luke picked up a stout pole from the sled and tramped over to a line of willow bushes, where he pounded the pole into the ground. Loud, brittle sounds of ice cracking rang through the air as he repeated the process in several spots. "Drink up, ladies."

He stepped back on the sled, the horses leaned into their harness, and the sled took off with a jerk. Slow to brace herself, J.J. fell backward. At the same instant Luke swung a bale of hay from the sled. The hay bale connected with J.J.'s side, pitchforking her to the ground. J.J. took one look at the advancing cows and struggled to regain her feet.

Strong arms plucked her from the hay-strewn ground and hauled her back onto the sled. "At this rate, I'm never going to finish feeding," Luke said.

"You're the one who insisted I come, and it's not my fault you made me wear all these clothes. I can hardly move."

"I won't argue you move a whole lot—" he paused "—better when you're wearing less."

J.J. ignored the reference to her earlier nakedness. "Admit it. You insisted I come this morning because you knew I know absolutely nothing about ranching and animals. You expected me to make a fool of myself."

"If you knew that, why did you come along?"

"Not because you ordered me. Since I'm forced," she accentuated the word, "to be here, I may as well learn what I can about ranching. It's still a fairly major industry in Colorado, and a little knowledge might come in handy at the law firm."

"Nice to know I'm good for something." Luke guided the team across the pasture, repeated the gate procedure and headed back toward the ranch buildings. "I'm surprised you admit it. As fond as you are of refusing to accept help from a mere male."

"Let me guess. I said I could have handled myself with Birdie's husband, so your nose is out of joint. Why can't men admit a woman can be competent and capable?"

"Why can't a woman—a person—admit a man might be bigger and stronger than her—or him?" he countered. "When a bully is picking on someone smaller, I react. If Parker had been shoving around a smaller guy, I would have interfered. Is that so hard for you to accept?"

"How would you like me constantly rushing to your rescue? You wouldn't like it, because you'd think I thought you were weak and incapable of taking care of yourself."

"Be reasonable, O'Brien. I'm taller, heavier and stronger than you. You wouldn't stand a chance if I attacked you."

"Is that right, Mr. Macho Man? I believe brains can win over brawn every time." If Luke hadn't laughed, she wouldn't have been tempted to demonstrate. She gave him a sweet smile. "May I drive the horses?"

"Sure. Doesn't require much. Hondo and Johnny know the way home. Here. Hold the reins like this," he placed them in her hands, "and don't pull tight."

J.J. moved past the center of the sled so Luke was forced to stand on the edge. "This is fun," she said disingenuously.

Balancing on his wide-spread feet, not bothering to hold on to the sled, Luke smiled a very patronizing smile. His smile tipped the scales against him. Anyone who smiled that way deserved a lesson in brainpower over muscles.

The sled hit a small bump and lurched slightly. J.J. immediately threw herself off balance, gripping the sled with one hand as she rammed an elbow into Luke's midriff. He tumbled very satisfactorily from the sled. J.J. slapped the reins against the horses' rumps. "Giddyup, you two. Home, Hondo, Johnny. Home! Move it!" The horses obligingly broke into a shambling trot.

They didn't trot fast enough.

J.J. flew from the sled, dropping the reins at the unexpected attack. She'd barely assimilated Luke had grabbed her before she careened into his solid body. They fell into the ditch beside the road, the heavy snow cushioning their landing. The sled and horses disappeared down the road. J.J. wiped snow from her face. "You big oaf, get off me. The horses are running away."

Luke shifted his body, but an arm and thigh kept her pinned in place. "They're headed to the barn. They'll wait there until someone takes care of them. Meanwhile, I think we were discussing brains versus brawn."

"I don't want to talk about it anymore." J.J. hated losing.

"Good. Neither do I."

J.J. forgot the cold snow beneath her at the scorching gleam in Luke's eyes. His slow smile turned her insides to slush. Even icy cold, his lips set her blood on fire. He tasted of morning coffee and toothpaste. Luke wedged his arm under her head. She felt his other arm moving, heard the sound of a glove being removed, and then his hand slid beneath the heavy coat she wore. Warmth penetrated J.J.'s multiple layers of sweaters, from her waist, up her rib cage, to an aching breast. She sighed with pleasure into their kiss. Luke settled a leg between her thighs. Remembering how she'd loved touching Luke's silken smooth skin and running her fingers along rippling muscles, J.J. wanted to strip off his jacket and warm her hands against his bare back.

Luke raised his head a couple of inches. "You make me crazy," he said, his breath puffing warmly against her face.

"I make you crazy?" J.J. blinked snow from her lashes. "I'm buried in snow, wearing clothes that don't belong to me, kissing a man I have nothing in common with, a man I intend to divorce. Not to mention it's broad daylight, and we're on a country road where anyone could come along any minute." She had absolutely no desire to move. "Sensible people don't do things like this."

"We bring out the worst in each other." He lowered his head.

"Absolutely," J.J. muttered into the mouth closing over her own. His tongue bathed the inside of her mouth with moist heat. His hand, still beneath her coat, warmed her other breast. She'd break off their kiss in a second. In their short time of cohabitation, he'd learned how she liked to be kissed. He demonstrated that knowledge until her whole body quivered. His thumb grazed the hard tip of her breast.

Snow covered the ground. The temperature was probably a hundred below zero. J.J. wanted to remove her clothes and feel Luke pressed against her, bare flesh to bare flesh.

Luke slid his lips from her mouth. "Your face is frozen," he said against her cheek. He lifted his head. Desire and rueful amusement mingled in his eyes. "If we don't get up right now, I'm going to rip both our clothes off, and we're going to end up with frostbite in places we could never explain.''

Luke stood, then pulled her to her feet. Briskly he brushed the snow from her clothing. Gradually his movements slowed, the brushing becoming more caressing than utilitarian. J.J. closed her eyes and leaned into his hands, her body craving even this touch. Luke pressed a hard, quick kiss on her lips, then climbed up to the road, pulling her along.

J.J. spoke as they walked beneath the ranch gate. ''This is all your fault. I'd be okay if you'd quit kissing me. I don't want to want you.''

''You don't have to kiss me back.'' The icy snow crunched under Luke's boots.

She knew she didn't have to kiss him back. Her mouth apparently did not. ''I don't love you. Don't take this personally, but you're just a sex object to me.''

''Do me a favor, O'Brien,'' Luke said harshly. ''Quit reminding me you want to go to bed with me, or I won't be responsible for my actions.''

J.J. slogged through the snow. ''My coming here was a mistake. We're making things worse. You know we're incompatible. We want different things from life. We would never have made a go of our marriage.'' J.J. stopped, freeing the hand Luke still held. ''The best thing is for me to call Burton to come and take me home.''

''No. We made a deal.'' He faced her, his hands resting on his hips. ''I may not be a lawyer, but I'm sure oral contracts are as binding as written ones.''

J.J. met his steady gaze with troubled eyes. He was wrong about oral contracts, but that was the least of her concerns. She wanted to run. She wanted to find a warm corner of the barn where they could make love. She didn't know what she wanted. Her lungs filled with cold, dry air. Burton was right to insist she come. Even if it meant staying here three weeks, she had to find the key for breaking the spell Luke held over her. "I'll stay. But I think we ought to keep out of each other's way as much as we can while I'm here."

Shaking his head, Luke tipped up her face with a glove-clad hand. "That's the worst thing we can do. All we have between us now are bedroom memories. To change that, we need to spend as much time together as we can. Unless we're sleeping, I want you glued to my side. By the end of three weeks we won't be able to stand the sight of each other."

Maybe by the end of three weeks. J.J. furtively eyed Luke as they drove into town. Now, however, he looked sexy as all get out, from his worn boots to his wide-brimmed hat. The parts in between weren't bad, either. Long, leg-hugging, faded jeans, sheepskin jacket over wide shoulders. A strong-jawed profile as he squinted into the intense sunlight reflecting off the snow.

From this angle she couldn't see the cleft in his already beard-shadowed chin. This morning his shaving brush and mug had been sitting by the sink when she'd used the bathroom. The smell of his soap had haunted the bathtub-shower enclosure.

Luke rubbed his hand over his chin. "What? Did I miss a spot shaving?" He didn't turn his head but continued to concentrate on his driving. A snowplow had been over the road leaving a sheet of ice beneath a scraped layer of snow.

He'd felt her staring at him. J.J. reluctantly moved her eyes from his profile and gazed resolutely out the window. Something in the distance caught her attention. "What are those animals? They look like elk. At least a hundred of them."

"A good-size herd winters there on Sentinel Mountain."

J.J. watched the elk until she could no longer see them, then scanned the rest of the countryside. The road bridged willow-lined streams and passed ranches of varying sizes. It was easy to see why this area was called a park. The land stretched flatly until it bumped up against mountains on all sides. "Has your family been here a long time?"

"My mom's family has. The earliest Stirling came over in the late 1800s. He was a second son, seeking his fortune. Lots of English aristocrats bought up land in the west and ran cattle on it, but most of them went back home and left an American, a Westerner, here in charge. The English lords returned now and again to hunt, but that was pretty much it. Stirling was different. He not only stuck around, but he married his partner's daughter. By the time I came along, the ranch belonged to Zane and my mom. She owns forty-five percent, but leaves the running of it to me, since Zane left me his share."

"Is your dad from around here, too?"

"No, he comes from a military family, went to West Point. My mom met him when she went back east to college."

"And your uncle never married?"

"He married. A college girl my mom brought home on one of their vacations. His wife spent more time visiting back east than she did on the ranch. When she was here, she spent the whole time trying to convince Zane to move back east, said her dad could get him a job in the family business. She never understood Zane's feeling for the ranch. They divorced after eighteen months. Zane never blamed her. Said it was his own fault for marrying a woman not born and bred to the ranch."

"You weren't born and bred to the ranch."

He laughed shortly. "That was my mom's fault, which I did my best to rectify. Mom and I lived here during my dad's two tours of Vietnam, and after that, I couldn't get enough of ranch living. I spent every summer here from the time I was six. When I got in trouble one time too many in Europe, my folks shipped me back here for my last two years of high school." He smiled wryly. "Zane kept me so busy, I didn't have time to get in trouble here." He turned serious. "This was one place I didn't want to get banished from."

"You came here in high school and never left?"

"I left for a while. Look over there, on the ground." He slowed the pickup. "Sage grouse."

J.J. looked in the direction of his pointing finger. Large birds, ten of them, dark against the snow, pecked at the brush. If Luke hadn't pointed them out, she'd never have seen them, they blended in so well with their surroundings. Something she'd never be able to do here.

In town Luke dropped J.J. off and pointed to a diner down the street, instructing her to meet him in an hour. She wandered the short main street, stopping to browse in front of shop windows, reluctant to enter and run the awkward risk of having to introduce herself. Pickup trucks of all sizes, colors and ages patrolled the street. Occasionally a huge logging truck filled with long pine logs lumbered past. Her hour almost up, J.J. picked her way through the snow heaped down the center of the street. Luke pulled into the diner's parking lot ahead of her. He waited for her at the diner's door.

Tantalizing smells and hot, moist air enveloped them as they entered. A single counter ran the length of the diner, and several men sitting on tall stools turned at their entry and greeted Luke, eyeing J.J. curiously. A tall, slim woman in blue jeans and a faded red plaid shirt with her blond hair wrapped in a coronet of braids put two heavy white mugs on the counter in front of two empty stools. Steam poured from the mugs.

Luke hung his and J.J.'s coats on rustic hooks by the door and sat on one of the stools. J.J. sat beside him. "Susan," Luke said, "Meet J. J. O'Brien. O'Brien, this is Susan Curtis. Susan makes the best pies in Colorado."

J.J. made polite sounds as the woman laughed, displaying even white teeth in a beautiful, perfectly made-up face. The mirrored wall behind the woman reflected J.J.'s face, red and chapped from the cold. She ran her fingers through her short, ordinary brown hair, hair hopelessly matted down by her knit cap.

"Only in Colorado?" the woman said in a teasing voice, her marvelous blue eyes flashing at Luke. "Last fall you told some hunters I made the best pie in the world."

"Yeah, but your head got so swollen, the rest of us couldn't fit into this dinky little place to eat any pie. The town council made me promise not to say it again."

J.J. sipped her scalding coffee and wondered if Luke and this Susan knew how silly they sounded. The woman had no business smiling so coyly at a married man.

Luke turned to J.J. "A trip to town isn't complete without a piece of Susan's pie. What kind do you want?" He pointed to a small blackboard propped against an easel on the counter.

J.J. read her choices. Lunch seemed a distant memory. "Banana cream."

"Sorry. All gone." The woman didn't sound the least bit sorry. She slid a plate holding a huge piece of meringue pie in front of Luke. Slices of banana nestled in the creamy filling.

J.J. pretended not to notice and ordered apple pie.

Susan slapped the plate down in front of J.J. "How do you like North Park, Mrs. Remington? It's not much like Denver."

"No, it's not," J.J. said. Susan Curtis knew who she was. Knew, and from the tone of her voice, didn't much like it. Luke said he hadn't slept with another woman since they'd gotten married. Had he slept with Susan before his marriage? Had he confided in her the whole mess of his marriage and looked to her for sympathy? The way she flirted with him was disgraceful. No wonder the men sitting at the counter left.

As soon as the door closed behind them, Susan leaned on the counter in front of Luke. "Ad Parker was in here this morning, spouting off. Birdie's run off, and he's furious."

"Call the police if he bothers you."

"He's looking for her."

Luke shrugged and forked another piece of pie.

"He said when he finds out where she is, someone's going to be sorry," Susan said.

J.J.'s experience with clients told her the fewer people who knew where Birdie was, the better. Before Luke could divulge Birdie's whereabouts, J.J. dropped her fork. The tiny thud as it hit the vinyl-tiled floor reverberated around the small diner. "Sorry," she said. "Could I please trouble you for a clean fork?" When Susan silently handed her a fork, J.J. said, "Luke's right. This pie is wonderful. Have you lived here long, Susan?"

"Three years."

"You and Luke must be good friends."

"We haven't slept together if that's what you're asking."

Luke choked on his pie and grabbed his mug and drank deeply.

"I wasn't asking, but it's interesting you felt compelled to tell me. Luke's love life before he married me doesn't interest me," J.J. lied. "Luke isn't the type to be unfaithful." She had no idea how she knew that, but she would have bet five years' salary on it. She flushed as she saw Luke watching her in the mirror, his eyes narrowed as he contemplated her above his mug. She gave him a saccharine smile and concentrated on her pie.

Susan refilled their mugs. "Since we're speaking frankly, Mrs. Remington—"

"Call me J.J. And I use my own last name. O'Brien."

"As I was saying, Mrs. Remington, Luke's a damned fine man, and he deserves a damned fine woman."

"Susan, mind your own business," Luke said flatly.

"My friends are my business. And that's what Luke and I are, Mrs. Remington. Good friends. Very good friends. But we're not lovers, never have been lovers, and won't ever be lovers. You want to know something else?" She steamrollered over J.J.'s negative answer. "If I did want to roll in the hay with Luke, I wouldn't worry a second about competition from a cold-blooded, stuck-up city woman who thinks she's too good for him."

J.J. carefully put down her mug of coffee lest she fling the contents into the beautiful blue eyes coldly condemning her. "I'll wait for you in the truck, Luke." Stopping at the door to grab her coat, J.J. turned to face Susan Curtis. "You should worry about me, Ms. Curtis, because having rolled in the hay with me, as you so quaintly put it, Luke will never be satisfied with second-best. You'd find it extremely difficult to make him happy." She slammed the door on her way out.

Luke exited on her heels. "What the hell was that about?" he snarled, getting into the pickup.

J.J. snapped her seat belt shut and yanked her knit cap down over her ears. "Why ask me? You're the one who blabbed the details of your version of our marriage all over Colorado."

"Damn it, O'Brien." Luke clamped his hands on the steering wheel. "People wondered why I kept disappearing from the stock show last year. If I'd known you were going to kick me out days after our wedding, I wouldn't have told any of my friends I intended to marry you. People asked questions when I came back alone. I had to say something."

"That something being your cold-blooded, stuck-up city wife thought she was too good for you?" The cold made her nose run.

He manhandled the pickup out of the parking lot. "I said things didn't work out, so we separated. If Susan chose to put her own interpretation on the situation, it wasn't my doing.''

J.J. sniffed.

A slight wind had come up. Luke wrenched the pickup around a small drift of snow along the edge of the road. Silence reigned in the cab of the pickup. Finally Luke said, ''I thought you two would like each other.''

''I'm sure Susan is a delightful person. In fact, I have a brilliant idea. After I go back to Denver, you and Susan can come down and double-date with Burton and me.''

Two days later, faced with Burton's reproachful gaze from the bedside chest, J.J. continued to revamp Monday afternoon's scene in the diner so she came out less like a jealous harpy and Susan Curtis came out more like a troublemaking busybody.

Preoccupied with self-justification, at first J.J. paid scant attention to the voices coming from below. Then Birdie, her voice edged with hysteria, exchanged shouts with a loud, coarse-voiced man. J.J. sprang to her feet. Birdie's husband had returned. Starting down the stairs, J.J. heard a low rumble, which sounded like Luke. She debated what to do. The three in the kitchen wouldn't welcome her interference. Birdie's shrill scream froze J.J. halfway down the stairs.

Luke's voice traveled clearly from the kitchen. ''Put that away, Parker, before you do something you'll regret.''

J.J. slipped out of her shoes, and tiptoed down to the front hall. Detouring through Luke's office, she strained to hear how serious the situation in the kitchen was. If things had reached a critical stage, she'd phone 911 and report an emergency. On the other hand, if Luke had things under control, he wouldn't appreciate J.J. bringing the police into this.

Stealing softly to the office door, J.J. cautiously peeked around the corner. Ad Parker stood with his back to her, facing Luke. Parker was laughing, a most unpleasant sound. About ten feet from Parker, Luke leaned against the refrigerator, his thumbs in his jeans' side pockets. He might have been watching a mildly interesting sideshow. He didn't deceive J.J. for a minute. Even from the office doorway she could tell every muscle in Luke's body stood at attention. Waiting for something. For what?

J.J. looked and found Birdie. The younger woman sat on the floor near Ad Parker, huddled against a cupboard, her hands curved protectively around her stomach. A bright red patch the size and shape of a man's large hand colored her check. Her eyes were enormous as she stared fearfully up at her husband.

J.J. flicked her gaze back to Parker. Just then he moved his hand, gesturing. The ceiling light bounced off the huge knife he held in his hand. A knife pointed at Luke. Blood roared in J.J.'s head, blotting out the men's conversation. She retreated to Luke's office.

It was too late for 911. J.J. spun around, searching the room for a weapon. Anything to give Luke the edge. Words beat at her head. Hurry, hurry. How long before Parker got annoyed with Luke's refusal to show fear? How long before Parker interpreted Luke's indifferent attitude as the contempt for Parker it was? Panic clawing at her, she looked desperately around Luke's office again. No shotgun, no hand gun, no sword. J.J. grabbed the only things available and crept back toward the kitchen.

"Yessir, after I take care of you, Remington, I'll look for that sweet mouth you say you're married to." He slurred his words. "You've had Birdie, turnabout's fair play." Parker lashed backward with a booted foot at Birdie's involuntary gasp. Birdie crumpled to the floor.

Parker's knife pointed straight at him, Luke didn't so much as flinch. Only the muscle throbbing in Luke's jaw told J.J. how furious he was. She took a deep breath, said a silent prayer the floor didn't squeak and padded quietly into the kitchen.

Sobbing, her face buried in her arms, Birdie didn't see J.J. Luke's gaze passed over J.J. as if she were invisible. "My wife is a total idiot," Luke said in a bored voice. "Don't waste your energy."

J.J. almost tripped over her own feet. How dare he? Just in time she prevented herself from lambasting him. Were her brains addled? Luke was distracting Parker so Parker wouldn't see J.J. sneaking up behind him.

She was close enough to smell the alcohol Birdie's husband had obviously guzzled before he came. Her heart pounding so loudly she thought surely Parker must hear it, J.J. rammed her weapon into his back. At the same instant she bashed his knife hand with Luke's cordless phone, yelling, "Drop the knife!"

CHAPTER FIVE

LUKE slammed the office door behind them.

"I don't know why you're so annoyed." The sheriff had gone, taking a sullen Ad Parker with him. Birdie was tucked into bed. Adrenaline still surged through J.J.'s veins.

"I. Am. Not. Annoyed." His forbidding gaze pinned J.J. to the office sofa. "I am furious. Do you have any idea how close you came to getting one of us killed?"

"Killed! I rescued you! All you were doing was lolly-gagging against the refrigerator while Parker bullied you. You didn't blink an eye when he kicked Birdie." J.J. knew she was being unfair, but Luke wasn't being fair, either.

"I thought," Luke said from between clenched teeth, "Birdie would prefer cracked ribs to a knife sticking between them."

"With a little bit of effort, you could have prevented him from doing either. Parker was threatening you and Birdie with a knife, and I didn't see either of you putting up much of a fight. What was I supposed to do? Say, 'Excuse me, I need to start dinner. Could you take them and your knife into another room?'"

"Ev was on his way. I didn't go into the kitchen to start a war. I wanted to give Parker a target besides Birdie. He stopped hitting her when I went in because he thought having the upper hand over me a lot more fun."

"How was I supposed to know you'd called the sheriff before you went into the kitchen? You didn't give me any signal to back off or go away."

"I thought I was perfectly clear. I told you what you were doing was idiotic. I told you not to waste your energy."

"I didn't know you were talking to me."

"Would you have preferred I asked you what the hell you were doing sneaking up behind a drunken, armed man?"

"I was armed, too."

"Armed!" Luke turned and clamped his hands on the windowsill. Leaning his forehead against the frosted glass pane, he swore fluently before tossing cold words over his shoulder. "You were not armed. You had a telephone and a set of elk antlers."

"And the element of surprise."

Luke turned back to her, his rigid posture radiating anger. "I'm not getting through to you, am I? You think you're some kind of damned Texas ranger who rode in and saved the town. You're practically blowing the smoke off the ends of your six-shooters. You could have gotten one of us killed. If Parker hadn't dropped the knife and—"

"But he did drop the knife. Just as I intended when I hit his wrist with your phone."

"If he'd been holding the knife correctly, you could have dropped a piano on his wrist and, no matter how drunk he was, he wouldn't have let go of his knife. You think those damned antlers would have kept him off you for even a second? He'd have gone for you, and I would have been forced to rescue you. And if Parker and I got into a struggle for the knife, who knows what Birdie would have done?"

"None of those things happened, so I don't know why you're carrying on and on about something that's over and done with."

"I am not carrying on," he said through his teeth. "I am trying to get you to recognize that you recklessly endangered all of us. I had everything under control. I didn't need some hysterical female with heroic fantasies dashing to my rescue.''

J.J. bolted upright on the sofa. "That's what this is all about. I dented your masculine pride.''

"This has nothing to do with my masculine pride.''

"Of course it does. You can't handle the idea that I, a mere woman, got you, Mr. Macho Man, out of a jam. It's fine and dandy if you rush to my rescue, whether I need it or want it, but let me do something to help you and you go ballistic.''

"Do not turn this into a man-woman thing,'' Luke warned her coldly.

"I'm not. You are.'' J.J. thrust out her bottom lip in imitation of a pouting child and chanted, "All because the great big hairy cowboy can't bear to say 'thank you' to the little bitty woman who saved him from the bad guy.''

Luke stalked over to the sofa and leaned down, his hands gripping the back of the sofa on either side of J.J. "I can't believe,'' he said deliberately, "not one of your brothers has strangled you by now.''

J.J. blatantly fluttered her eyelashes at Luke. "Gosh, you're cute when you're mad.''

Luke straightened with a snap, yanking J.J. to her feet. Digging his fingers into her scalp, he held her head immobile as he plastered her mouth with a hard, possessive kiss.

J.J. returned his kiss with interest. This was what she needed. Intoxicated with the success of her rescue efforts, every cell in her body simmered with suppressed excitement. Kissing Luke released the pressure and kept her from boiling over. To the victor goes the spoils, she thought triumphantly, her lips parting as Luke deepened the kiss.

Sliding his hands down her back, he curved them around her bottom and lifted her from the floor. J.J. clutched his hair, refusing to relinquish his lips. Luke's laugh was strangled in the back of his throat and carried her across his office. Lowering her carefully to the wooden table, he wrapped her legs around his waist and slipped his hands under her heavy sweater.

Heat poured from every pore of J.J.'s body. A sensuous, writhing heat that eddied around her and Luke, binding them tighter and tighter together until she could barely distinguish where her body left off and Luke's rock-hard muscles and sinews began. Despite their clothing, J.J. felt the warmth of his body. He smelled of soap and outdoors. And intensely male.

Luke shifted, drawing J.J. nearer. His mouth left hers to travel over the planes of her face, leaving the searing imprint of his lips on every square centimeter of her facial skin. Beneath her sweater, he'd found the fastening to her bra. It opened as easily as the gate to his pasture, and Luke laid claim to her breasts.

The heady exhilaration of victory disappeared, replaced by emotions of quite another sort. J.J.'s bones melted away. Her head fell back, exposing the pulse at the base of her neck. Luke immediately pounced, his mouth relishing the shallow, rapid beating of her heart. Hot, callused palms cupped breasts heavy with longing. Thumbs circled the tips, never quite touching them, until J.J. thought she'd go mad. She pressed against his hands, and he caressed her nipples with knowing fingers. J.J.'s nails bit into Luke's shoulders.

He stilled, then removed his hands from her sweater. Reaching behind his back, he loosened her legs binding them together and took a single step backward. "That," he said in a harsh growl, "is the only man-woman thing between us."

J.J. wanted to slug him. Her entire body quivered with wanting him, but she had too much pride to beg a man to continue making love to her. Especially when the man made it clear he hadn't been making love, but had been teaching her some stupid object lesson. She'd be darned, no, she'd be damned, if she'd accept any lesson from Luke Remington. Shoving him aside, she jumped off the table. Only to promptly trip over one large booted foot and fall to the floor.

Ignoring her ineffective efforts to ward him off, Luke pulled her to her feet. He looked at her face and swore viciously for the second time since the sheriff had gone.

J.J. flinched at the darkness she glimpsed in his slitted eyes.

"No, O'Brien, don't." He ran a gentle finger over J.J.'s bottom lip. "It's swollen. I didn't mean to hurt you. It's just that you scared the hell out of me when you waltzed into the kitchen with those damned flimsy antlers. All I could see was Parker burying his knife in you." He cleared his throat. "Which doesn't give me the right to force a kiss on you—"

J.J. jammed her palm over Luke's mouth. "You stop right there, cowboy. If you don't want to kiss me, be man enough to say so. Don't insult me with garbage about forcing kisses on me. If that's your backhanded way of saying I should have been fighting you off, when we both know I was close to ripping off your clothes— ouch!" J.J. snatched back her hand and sucked on the smarting, tender flesh. "Why did you bite me?"

"Because you are driving me insane."

"Oh yeah?" she said inelegantly. "I'm not the one picking up hay bales so I'll have an excuse to flex my muscles. I'm not the one running around with blue jeans painted on my tight bottom. I'm not the one exuding pheromones every time he breathes."

Luke gave her a blank look, then burst out laughing. "Tight bottom?" He choked out the words. "Exuding pheromones?"

J.J. shrugged.

His laughter faded away, and Luke ruefully shook his head. "We're a pair. If I watched you floss your teeth,

I'd probably think it was the sexiest thing I'd ever seen a woman do.''

J.J. made a face. "Physical attraction is senseless. It makes me crazy. Anthony and Cleopatra. Helen and Paris. Incompatible, nothing in common, yet they caused wars. All because of hormones gone berserk.''

"Maybe if everyone had left them alone, their heated passions would have quickly burnt out," Luke said. "Cleo would have realized she preferred barges while Tony liked horses. Helen and Paris would have tired of the other always hogging all the mirrors.''

J.J. elaborated on Luke's scenario. "Tony would have thought Cleo wasn't much without all her makeup, and Cleo would have said Tony smelled of the stables. Paris and Helen would have accused the other of being vain and shallow and unfaithful.''

"You see? Proof positive." Luke grinned at J.J. "All they needed was to get the physical attraction out of their systems.''

Not easy if Anthony or Paris grinned anywhere near as sexily as Luke Remington grinned. J.J. hated the gooey feeling deep in the pit of her stomach. "I better throw something on for dinner. Rescuing cowboys makes me hungry." She fled to the kitchen.

A quick glance at the kitchen clock told her the hour was later than she'd realized. Dinner would have to be something quick. Forays to the pantry and the freezer in the basement yielded the makings for macaroni and cheese, hamburger patties, fruit salad and blueberry muffins. J.J. measured and mixed, but busy hands failed to keep her mind from dwelling on what had occurred between her and Luke.

They couldn't seem to keep their hands off each other. Every situation, no matter the emotion or events precipitating it, seemed to end with Luke kissing J.J. She grimaced and attacked the cheese with the grater. Saying Luke kissed J.J. didn't paint an accurate picture. He wasn't exactly kissing a block of wood. Not only had J.J. never pushed him away, but she welcomed his kisses. Most of the time it was difficult to know who was kissing whom. All J.J. knew was, she liked Luke's kisses.

Therein lay the problem. She didn't want to like Luke's kisses. She didn't want to like Luke. They had absolutely nothing in common. She stared out the window over the sink into the dark night beyond the enclosed back porch. Big, fluffy snowflakes danced around the tall ranch light poles. In Denver she'd have picked up dinner on the way home from work and be looking forward to an evening spent in front of her gas fireplace, curled up in a cozy chair studying briefs. She'd be anticipating weekend plans—dinner with Burton and Carrie, maybe a movie, or a concert or the theater. On Sunday she and Carrie could go to the mall.

The thought of spending the rest of her life on a ranch made J.J.'s blood run cold. She'd gone to college because she wanted to make a difference. She hadn't gone because her goal in life was to walk three steps behind some man. She wanted to be out front in the fight for justice. People who'd been second in their law class did not feed beef cows. They sued cash cows.

She put water for cooking the macaroni on to boil. Being Luke's wife meant giving up her career, her goals, her dreams. Being Burton's wife meant freedom to do what she'd always wanted to do. She had no difficulty choosing. Marriage to Luke was like eating cotton candy. Attractive, heavenly on the tongue and quickly over. Marriage to Burton was like... J.J. stared at the stovetop. Like macaroni and cheese. Not glamorous, but filling. Life-sustaining. The water in the pan boiled over.

J.J. reached for a dishrag and heard a low moan from down the hall. Switching off the stove burners, she hurried to Birdie's room.

It if weren't for the fact of her pregnancy, Birdie's

slender form would have been lost beneath the blankets she'd heaped over herself. She didn't stir. Either J.J. had imagined the sound, or the rising wind was playing tricks. She turned to tiptoe silently away without disturbing Birdie.

A small cry came from the bed. J.J. twisted around to see Birdie curl her body tightly in a fetal position. "Birdie, are you all right?" she asked softly, not sure if the young woman had cried out in her sleep. A husband like Ad Parker would give any woman nightmares.

Birdie's voice quavered with fear. "I think my baby's coming."

J.J.'s heart stopped; her mind went totally blank. Then reason asserted itself. "Have you called your doctor?"

"I was afraid to get out of bed."

"When is the baby due?"

"Two weeks."

J.J. thought a minute. "I don't think you're having your baby, Birdie. I remember my mom had false labor pains before she had my youngest brother." She filled her voice with reassurance. "The excitement with your husband probably got Junior's attention and he's a little restless. Lay here and rest and everything will be fine. I'll bring you a little dinner—macaroni and cheese— doesn't that sound good?"

Birdie moaned.

"I'll tell you what," J.J. suggested. "I'll get Luke's cordless phone in here and dial your doctor and you can talk to him. I'm sure he'll tell you bed rest is what you need."

"The bed's all wet down there. I'm afraid to look. J.J.—" Birdie's voice rose in panic "—what if I'm losing my baby?"

J.J. moved swiftly to the foot of Birdie's bed. "How about I check?" Without waiting for an answer, J.J. carefully pulled the blankets free from between the mattress and bedsprings and lifted them up. One look and

J.J. let out the breath she'd been holding. "Everything's fine, Birdie. Your water broke, and you're going to have a baby. You take it easy while I go tell Luke to call your doctor. I'll be right back."

Flashing Birdie a confident smile, J.J. walked from the room. She didn't break into a run until she was out of Birdie's sight and hearing. Luke was on the phone when she tore into his office. Grabbing the receiver from him, she slammed it on its base. "Birdie's going to have a baby."

"Damn it, J.J., I was talking to the sheriff. I know Birdie's going to have a baby. Did you have to— Oh hell, you mean she's having her baby right now?"

J.J. nodded her head, her mind searching frantically for the best way to cope with the urgent situation. "Call her doctor. Her water broke. Don't just sit there looking at me. Call her doctor. Call an ambulance. Call the sheriff. No, wait, what if we don't have time? We'll have to drive her. Go start your truck. No, call an ambulance first, then start your truck. We'll meet the ambulance halfway. Hurry up, call them. Move!"

Luke moved. Around his desk to clamp his hands on J.J.'s shoulders. "Take a deep breath and calm down."

"Calm down! Didn't you hear what I said? Birdie's having her baby. Right now!"

"Your panicking isn't going to help anything. I'm sure Birdie has lots of time. Relax."

"I'm not panicking." J.J. tore out of his grip and dashed back down the hall. Outside Birdie's room, she skidded to a stop, and counted to ten. Wiping her trembling palms down her side, she pinned a smile on her face and walked into the room. Birdie lay on her side, her body curled into a tight ball.

"Luke's calling your doctor, and everything's going to be fine." J.J. tried to think of the shows she'd seen where a woman gave birth. Granted, they gave birth Hollywood style, but they couldn't be too far wrong, could they? Didn't they have to have experts around when they filmed or something?

"Why don't we see if we can make you more comfortable. How about a clean nightgown?" J.J. moved over to the dresser and started opening drawers. She found a faded flannel gown in the second drawer. "This looks like just the thing to greet a new little human being in. Think you can scoot over here…?" J.J. abandoned the rest of her question as Birdie grabbed her hand and squeezed incredibly hard.

By the time Luke knocked on the bedroom door, J.J. had managed to put clean, dry sheets on the bed and get Birdie into a clean nightgown.

"How's everyone in here?" Luke asked.

"Well." J.J. divided her beaming smile between Birdie and Luke. "We're going to have a baby, Luke." She swallowed hard. "Real soon."

"I'll go get the pickup warmed up."

"I don't think we're going to need the pickup. It seems this baby has decided he wants to be born right here."

Luke frowned. "I think—"

J.J. smiled wider. "It doesn't matter what you think. We have a very impatient baby here." She plumped the pillows behind Birdie's head. "Remember what I said, Birdie. Breathe in and out, real deep and slow. That's the way. I'll bet yours isn't the first baby born in this house. Isn't this exciting? Think what a story you'll have to tell your son or daughter. Who knows? Breathe deep, Birdie, breathe. Thatta girl. Maybe having a lawyer around when you give birth is some kind of good luck omen. Your baby could grow up to be a Supreme Court Justice or something. Maybe I'll get to argue a case in front of her. Wouldn't that be something? Breathe, Birdie."

"J.J., can I see you in the kitchen a minute?"

J.J. gave Birdie a smile that stretched back to her molars. "I'll be right back. Luke probably wants dinner. Men. Don't forget to breathe deeply."

The smile disappeared before J.J. made it through the bedroom door. In the kitchen, she didn't give Luke a chance to speak. "When's the ambulance going to get here? Did you tell them to hurry? I think this baby is coming any minute."

"Have you looked out the window lately? It's snowing like a son of a gun out there," Luke said patiently. "If this turns into a full-scale blizzard, I don't know when or if the ambulance will get here."

"They have to get here. They have to." Hearing the alarm in her voice, she squeezed her eyes shut and clenched her fists at her side. After a minute, she opened her eyes, and asked, "What are we going to do?"

"Wash your hands. I'll call the hospital and tell them the situation. If need be, I can relay their instructions to you."

"Instructions to me? For what? Delivering a baby? Don't be ridiculous. Call your ranch hands' wives. Jeff's wife, Donna, may not be much older than Birdie, but Becky, Dale's wife, has two toddlers. Call her. She can make it across the ranch yard even if it is snowing."

Luke shook his head. "I called. Becky's in town at her mother's. Dale said he'd already talked to her and told her not to try coming home tonight in case the weather worsens."

"I'm not going to deliver a baby." The thought of being responsible for two human lives terrified J.J. Not that she'd admit it to Luke. "I know nothing about it. If I screw it up, Birdie could sue me." A faint outcry and the sound of her name coming from the bedroom knotted J.J.'s stomach.

"Birdie won't sue, and you won't screw up." Luke guided her over to the faucet and turned on the water. "Don't worry. You're doing fine in there."

"Fine!" J.J. swiveled away from the faucet, her wet

hands dripping on the floor. "I'm babbling a bunch of nonsense I heard on television. I'm not going to deliver a baby."

"You're going to deliver a baby." Luke grabbed a clean towel from the drawer and gently dried J.J.'s hands. "I'll get the hospital on the phone."

J.J. stood rooted to the floor in front of the kitchen sink. "You must have delivered hundreds of cows and horses. This won't be any different. You deliver the baby, I'll talk on the phone."

Luke corralled her face between his large hands. "I'll do what I can, but I think Birdie would prefer a woman. You're always claiming you're competent and capable and don't need a man rushing to your rescue. Put your money where your mouth is, O'Brien."

"This has nothing to do with whether I'm a competent person or not. I simply don't have the knowledge or expertise to safely deliver Birdie's baby."

Luke lightly kissed her lips, then turning her around, gave her a slight push in the direction of Birdie's bedroom. "Go welcome your Supreme Court Justice."

J.J. stopped at the room's threshold, gathered her composure and fixed a smile on her face. "How we doing in here?" she asked, filling her voice with cheer as she entered the room.

Birdie tried to return J.J.'s smile, a weak effort quickly curtailed as she let out a wail.

J.J. grabbed the younger woman's hand and uttered soothing gibberish. Birdie's pain seemed to last an eternity. A few crushed hand bones were irrelevant.

At last the younger woman sank, exhausted, back against the pillows. "I'm sorry. I don't mean to holler, but it hurt."

"Yell all you want," J.J. said. She wiped Birdie's sweating face with a paper tissue.

"I've got help on the phone," Luke said from outside

the room. "He wants to know how far apart the con-
tractions are and how long they last."

"How am I supposed to know—" Birdie's cry cut off
J.J.'s words. J.J. felt as exhausted as Birdie when the
pain finally eased. "I hope he timed that," J.J. snapped
over her shoulder.

"He wants to know if you can see anything."

"See anything? Like what? Oh." J.J. disengaged her
hand from Birdie's frenzied grip and moved further
down the bed and lifted the blankets from Birdie's legs.
She had to try twice before she could force the words
from her arid mouth. "I think I see the top of a baby's
head."

Birdie started screaming again.

J.J.'s heart lodged in her throat. "Luke, Luke, oh, oh,
oh, Luke…"

He was beside her, the phone pressed to his ear as he
relayed instructions. "Okay, O'Brien, gently guide, no
pulling, there, his head, hold him gently under the chin,
support his head, okay, here he comes, okay, okay, okay,
fella, okay, doing good, Birdie, okay, okay!" The last
came as an exultant shout.

The baby's lusty cry filled the bedroom.

In a blur J.J. took the twine Luke handed her, tied the
umbilical cord twice and cut between the twine with the
scissors Luke assured her he'd sterilized. She gently
wiped out the baby's mouth with her finger and cleaned
his nose. A warm rag appearing in her hand, she wiped
off the baby's face, smiling down at unfocused blue
eyes.

In spite of the pointed head, wrinkled face and the
disgusting glop covering the baby's body, J.J. thought
the infant the most beautiful, wondrous creature she'd
ever seen.

Birdie was crying and asking questions that could
barely be heard over the sound of the squalling infant.

The baby started shivering. Instinctively J.J. pulled the

covers from Birdie, ripped open her nightgown and gently laid the baby facedown on his mother's chest. She folded the nightgown and then the covers over mother and child.

"He's beautiful, Birdie." So beautiful, tears welled in J.J.'s eyes.

Birdie smiled wearily down at her new son. "He is beautiful. Thank you, J.J."

Luke cleared his throat. "Um, he's a she."

As one, Birdie and J.J. lifted the blankets and inspected the baby. Both broke into giggles.

"I didn't even notice," J.J. said.

Birdie stiffened. "J.J., another one!"

J.J. hurried to check. "Not a baby."

Luke stood by Birdie's head, watching mother and child. "I imagine it's the afterbirth."

"Oh," J.J. said. "There, now I think we're done. Luke, a towel, I guess." She bundled it between Birdie's legs as a thunderous pounding sounded at the front of the house.

"That's one healthy set of lungs." The first man into the bedroom beamed at Birdie. "Sounds like you went ahead without us." He slapped a blood pressure cuff on Birdie as a second man headed for the baby.

Too many people crowded the room and sucked the oxygen from the air. The blood drained from J.J.'s head, and she stumbled into the kitchen. Voices from the bedroom barely penetrated the fog smothering her brain. She washed her hands and flopped down on the nearest kitchen chair. Behind her metal clanged; male voices asked questions; Birdie answered softly; wheels squeaked. The infant screamed lustily.

J.J. sensed movement behind her, the sounds traveled down the hall, and then the front door opened and closed. Silence settled over the house.

J.J. looked down at her trembling hands. She'd done it. She'd delivered Birdie's baby. Not that Birdie had required all that much help, when it came right down to it. Still, in spite of the fact J.J. had been more terrified than she'd ever been in her life, she'd hung in there and delivered the baby. Triumph and satisfaction surged through her body. She wanted to stand up and shout at the top of her lungs.

Footsteps came down the hall.

J.J. glanced down at the filthy front of her clothes and jumped up to grab the large apron hanging on a hook near the stove. She slipped her head through the top opening as Luke entered the kitchen.

He stepped behind her and tied the apron strings at her waist, then rested his hands on her shoulders. "You did good work in there, O'Brien."

"And people say watching television is a waste of time. Hungry?" She switched on stove burners and shuffled pans. "Everything's almost ready. I don't know about you, but I'm starving. I hope they feed poor Birdie at the hospital. She never did get dinner." The water boiled and J.J. dumped the macaroni into the pan.

Luke pulled the cheese and grater toward him to finish up the task Birdie's baby had interrupted. "I'm serious. You done good, O'Brien. Shucks, now I know what you're capable of, I'd even trust you with my favorite cow."

"Cow!" She spun around. "You can't compare a human life to a—" The teasing light in Luke's eyes stopped her. "Beast," she said appreciatively. "She was a beautiful baby, wasn't she?"

"Beautiful? I didn't want to say anything in front of Birdie, but I've never seen such an ugly kid. That red face and pointed head... Birdie put on a good show, but she must have been sick at going through all that for a scrawny, shriveled peanut."

J.J. smiled. "Most babies look like that when they're first born. In a month she'll look totally different."

"How come you're suddenly the expert on babies?"

Luke asked, setting plates and eating utensils on the kitchen table.

"I have two younger brothers and two nephews—" she stirred cheese and milk into the drained pasta "—but believe me, changing diapers and delivering babies are poles apart."

"You've actually changed diapers?"

"And I'm darned good at it," she said in a challenging voice, sitting across from him at the table. "My nephews are four and six now. They don't care if I'm 'just a girl.' All they care about when they come to visit is I know where to buy good pizza and I take them to the zoo and the amusement park and to watch the Rockies play baseball. Why are you looking at me like that?"

He shook his head, not answering. "What's your favorite ride at the amusement park?"

"We like the merry-go-round the best. Quinlin, he's the oldest, insists on a black horse. Keefe doesn't care about color." She grinned. "Their eyes would bug out if they saw Hondo and Johnny. We'll have to take a picture of me beside them—without your uncle's coat on—to send to the boys."

"Sure." Luke asked questions about the rest of the family.

J.J. found herself telling him about the unending competition between herself and her brothers. "Mom and Dad treated us as equals. There was none of this girls do the dishes while the boys mow the lawns. I grew up shooting hoops, digging my own fishing worms, arguing politics at the dinner table. It wasn't until I got to school I learned girls were supposed to sit quietly with their hands folded while boys shouted out the answers and got all the attention. My brothers always let me tag along after them but, of course, their friends didn't want a girl hanging around."

"I expect that changed."

"In high school," J.J. said with a sigh. "Suddenly I

couldn't move without tripping over those same boys. Not because of my athletic abilities or my brain. Because of my stupid face. My introduction to the realization the world thinks anyone with a halfway pretty face must be a total bimbo.''

"I'll bet you were class queen, prom queen, queen of everything.''

"You'd lose the bet. The boys bored me. The girls resented me for disdaining what they wanted. I took refuge in books and finished high school in three years.'' She added glumly, "Class valedictorian.''

Luke helped her stack the dirty dishes in the dishwasher. "With all the doctors in your family, I'm surprised you didn't go into medicine and become a doctor or a nurse.''

"I always wanted to be a corporate lawyer, a mover and shaker. It must have been all those dinnertime political discussions. Besides, every woman doctor I knew was a gynecologist or a pediatrician. My mom's a nurse and wanted me to go into nursing. Nothing against nurses, but I didn't want to spend the rest of my life having men tell me what to do.''

Luke laughed. "You sound like my sister Sara.''

"I didn't know you had a sister.''

"Two, both pilots in the air force. Mick, Michelle, is in a C-5 squadron in Delaware. She met her husband, Far, when they were at the air force academy. Sara, she's three years younger than Mick, flies 141's out of Travis AFB in California.''

J.J. looked at Luke in astonishment. "You have two sisters who are fighter pilots?''

"Not fighter pilots. Right now they think they'd like to be, but I imagine when Far and Mick decide to start a family, Mick will resign her commission. And Sara will settle down once she meets the right man.''

"You mean they'll both give up their careers and stay home to be good little housewives?'' J.J. asked sweetly.

"My mother says her career was taking care of my dad and us kids. She followed Dad without complaint, and made a home for us wherever we lived, whatever the conditions. She didn't call it a sacrifice—she called it a privilege," he said stiffly.

"Is that what she wants for your sisters? To be a private maid and mistress to some man?"

"She sure as hell doesn't want them dying in the trenches with a bunch of men."

"That has nothing to do with their gender. She wouldn't want you dying in the trenches. Just because you think women are incapable of protecting you, doesn't mean they are."

Luke gave her a narrow-eyed look. "If I'm ever in a really tight spot, I can't think of two people I'd rather have on my side than Mick and Sara." He walked out of the kitchen.

Leaving J.J. staring after him in total astonishment. Luke Remington admitting he'd accept help from a woman? Sure, he'd accepted help from J.J. when it came to delivering Birdie's baby, but delivering babies was an area most men assumed women held the patent on. Like her brothers, much of the time Luke probably forgot his sisters were female.

When Ad Parker had threatened him with a knife, Luke had practically thrown a temper tantrum about J.J. coming to Luke's aid. Luke was no different than the boys in high school. He didn't care one iota about J.J.'s brains and abilities. All he wanted was to go to bed with her.

He wasn't about to get what he wanted.

CHAPTER SIX

"O'BRIEN, wake up, O'Brien."

J.J. opened her eyes. Luke's nose was inches from hers. "What?" Dregs of sleep clogged her brain.

"You were having a nightmare. You kept hollering 'no.'" He sat on the edge of her bed.

Bits and pieces of her dream flashed back, and her heart drummed against her rib cage. "I was delivering Birdie's baby, and everything went wrong," she said, groggy with sleep. "The baby wasn't a baby at all, but a huge horse, and it had antlers. And the antlers turned into knives and Birdie kept screaming her baby was dead and I didn't know what to do and her husband kept telling me I was a lawyer not a doctor and I was killing her baby and killing her and all I was wearing was an apron and Parker kept walking behind me and I knew I needed to find you but I couldn't remember where the barn was and I looked and looked..." J.J. jammed her fist into her mouth, biting down on her knuckle to stop the torrent of words.

Luke rescued her hand. "It's okay, O'Brien."

His words didn't make a dent in her nightmare-fogged mind. "Before I went to sleep I lay here thinking of all the disastrous things that could have happened. It could have been a breech birth, or the cord could have wrapped itself around the baby's neck, or I could have dropped her." Horrible images kept replaying in her mind, and without thinking, she rolled toward him, getting a death grip on the arm closest to her. "What if Birdie had hemorrhaged to death? Or the baby hadn't started crying? And don't babies go blind if you don't clean their eyes?

95

and I don't remember if I cleaned her eyes. Why was she crying so much? Did I hurt her when she was born? I don't think I pulled on her, but maybe I did? Maybe I hurt her neck. She could be paralyzed, and it would be all my fault.''

''O'Brien—''

''I know, people deliver babies all the time, I keep telling myself prehistoric women had babies, Native American women and pioneer women had babies, peasant women had babies in the fields, I should quit worrying about it, but every time I shut my eyes— What are you doing?'' She woke suddenly to full awareness as Luke stood and picked her up in a cascade of blankets.

He kicked the blankets out of his way. ''Trying to get some sleep.'' Carrying J.J. across the hall, he dumped her in the middle of his unmade bed.

His sheets retained the slightest hint of warmth where he'd been laying. ''I can't sleep here,'' J.J. protested.

''Apparently you can't sleep across the hall.'' Luke walked around the bed. ''At least this way when you start screaming as if you're about to be murdered, I won't freeze to death running to see if you're okay.'' Hauling back the down comforter, he crawled into the bed and pulled J.J. over next to him. ''You know I called the hospital and Birdie and her daughter are doing fine. The excitement's over. Go to sleep.''

She drew comfort from Luke's warm body. A weakness she regretted and would never admit to him. ''It's easy for you to be blasé. You've probably delivered hundreds of cows and horses, but I've never delivered so much as a puppy. Not that I was scared or anything. I don't get scared, not even when I didn't want to ride on the roller coaster, and Blaine said girls were always afraid to ride them and I said I wasn't afraid and I rode it and the next two days I couldn't move my neck because it was so sore but that wasn't because I was scared, and when I took the exam to get into law school and took my law boards I didn't throw up after both tests because I was scared so it must have been something I ate and—''

Luke wrapped his arms around her, pushing her face into his chest. "Are you going to talk all night?"

J.J. twisted her head around so she could breathe and blew his chest hair away from her nose. "No, I'm not, really I'm not, it's just I've never done anything like delivering a baby before, a human being, a live baby, and I—''

Luke's palm cut off the flow of words. "There's only one way to shut you up—'' he tugged her body toward the head of the bed so her face was level with his "—isn't there?"

She shook off his hand. "I'm sorry, I'll be quiet. I won't say another word, I promise...you go ahead and go to sleep, I'll be as quiet as a mouse...you won't hear another word from—''

Luke's mouth swallowed the rest of her promise.

The touch of his lips against hers had the same effect as a match tossed into a pile of dry grass. J.J. plastered herself against Luke's hard, muscled body, greedily devouring his kisses. She'd been assaulted by a full complement of emotions today, most of which she'd been forced to suppress or contain. There was no thought of denying herself now. She neither knew nor cared which of them ripped off his pajama bottoms or her nightgown. She only knew she couldn't abide anything between them.

Animals mating in the wild demonstrate cautious restraint. Luke and J.J. loved each other with a fierce intensity that knew no rules and allowed no holding back. Afterward, J.J. lay sated, yet drained, an odd combination, but one that described her state perfectly. "The state of well-being," she said drowsily.

Luke murmured an agreement, before adjusting her

body to fit against him. Then he slept, a hand laying claim to one of her breasts.

J.J. nestled against him, unabashedly seeking to share his body heat as she struggled to corral her thoughts, to think about what she'd done. She hadn't succumbed as much as she'd met Luke head-on. A tiny laugh tickled her throat. Body-on was more apt. Even as she thought about it, her nipple swelled to press against Luke's palm. His hand tightened possessively.

Her legs lay entangled with his, the hair on his legs rasping against the sensitive skin behind her knees. J.J. wiggled closer to him, molding her bottom into the curve of his hips. He smelled of soap and after-shave. And of their wedding night. The soporific sound of his deep breathing soothed J.J., and her eyelids drifted downward. It was impossible to control her thoughts or her body when she was so exhausted.

Luke shifted in his sleep; his hand trailed from her breast down to her stomach where it lay flat and warm against her skin. J.J.'s backbone melted into his chest and belly. She needed sleep. Tomorrow she'd be clear-headed. Tomorrow would be soon enough to deal with the ramifications of their lovemaking.

A hand roving over her body, renewing its familiarity with her secrets, awakened J.J. Moonlight bouncing off the snow lit the room and silhouetted Luke's wide shoulders as he sprawled at her side, his head propped on his other hand.

"You respond to me even in your sleep," he said with quiet satisfaction.

Once she'd believed he held the key to a side of her few knew. He hadn't, but at least he knew this about her, and she began to burn beneath his knowledgeable touch, her breathing turning rapid and shallow. His head backlit by moonlight, her eyes half closed, she couldn't read his face. Or guess his thoughts. Any messages flowed from his fingertips to her body. When she could stand the sweet torment no longer, she pulled him down on top of her. He came without hesitation, with a low laugh of triumph. To punish him, she captured his tongue between her teeth. And then the fire consumed them again.

Dawn grayed the room when J.J. awoke. She lay alone in the center of Luke's king-size bed. The chilly air in the room sent her burrowing further under the thick comforter. This being the first time she'd been in Luke's room, she unabashedly indulged her curiosity. As in the office, books and magazines lay in haphazard heaps on every flat surface. Boots spilled out of the half-open closet, a pair of jeans had been flung across the back of a ragged overstuffed chair, and a damp towel hung over one of the bottom bedposts. Faded cowboy print bark cloth from the forties curtained the windows. Pictures, probably from old calendars and framed in aged barn wood, hung on the walls. J.J. guessed the room, with the exception of the bed, had been decorated by Luke's grandmother about fifty years ago.

Stretching under the covers, J.J. felt the pull of muscles used after long inactivity. She wondered why Luke had left without wakening her. Out of kindness, to allow her to sleep longer? Or out of embarrassment? She welcomed not having to face him yet. Too many issues had to be resolved in her mind before she dealt with whatever he was thinking.

The first issue, of course, was their divorce. Last night changed nothing. She couldn't be the kind of wife Luke wanted. The physical side of their marriage had never been the problem. In bed, they were good together. She had no doubt once she got into bed with Burton, it would be good between them, too. She might not feel the same thrill now when Burton kissed her, but Burton had been married. He was experienced, and he would have no trouble igniting J.J.'s passions every bit as satisfactorily as Luke did.

It didn't take a genius to understand what had prompted her and Luke's actions last night. When it came to pent-up emotion, sex acted as a time-honored release and restorative.

Those two issues satisfactorily dealt with, J.J. contemplated the last issue with less equanimity. Unlike the others, this issue refused to go away or be boxed up with easy explanations. How did a woman look her almost ex-husband in the eye the morning after a night of unbridled passion? Even more difficult, how did she explain, despite having no regrets, she had no intention of repeating the incident?

An eternity spent showering failed to produce any magic answers. Heading down to the kitchen to see if Luke had eaten breakfast, J.J.'s sentiments careened from feeling it would be best to get the situation resolved to hoping Luke was nowhere around.

He sat at the kitchen table eating hot cereal and toast and reading a newspaper. "Good morning."

"Morning." Flustered by his presence and uncertain how to act, J.J. concentrated on pouring a cup of coffee. "Any word from the hospital?" She injected her voice with impersonal cheerfulness and looked at Luke's ear. His ears stuck out from his head the tiniest bit. Nothing about them should make her stomach feel funny. Nothing did, she told herself forcefully. That hollow feeling had to do with how little she'd managed to eat last night when she'd finally sat down to supper.

"Mother and daughter both doing fine. Want to run over and see them later today?"

"I'd like that."

"We'll go after I feed." Luke pushed back his chair and stood up. "About last night. As far as I'm concerned, nothing happened." He put his dirty dishes in the sink, his back to J.J. "There's no reason to bore Alexander with it. I know you had a rough day yesterday. You needn't worry I'll mention last night again or make any demands of you on account of it.'' He walked from the kitchen.

Leaving J.J. staring openmouthed after him. After a minute, she lifted the lid from the pan on the stove. Cooked oatmeal. She filled a bowl with the singularly unappetizing-looking mess. Luke's rush to excuse her from future appearances in his bed made it clear not repeating last night's lovemaking called for no sacrifice on his part.

Not that she wanted to share his bed. Admittedly it would have been nice if he'd allowed her to reject him first, but one couldn't have everything. She was thrilled she wouldn't have to worry about him importuning her to sleep with him.

The explanation behind his lack of interest suddenly struck her. Luke had said from the first he'd insisted she come here because he knew having her around would cure him of wanting her. A canary yellow coward, he'd called her, unfit to live on the ranch, who'd whine and complain and be an absolute pain in the neck. She hadn't fooled him yesterday. She'd done every one of those things. More concerned with her own stupid fears than with Birdie and the baby. Then, when it was all over, going to pieces in her bed and disturbing Luke. He probably figured having sex with her was the quickest way to settle her down so he could get some sleep. Her behavior had definitely killed all feelings Luke had ever had for her.

J.J. emptied her oatmeal down the garbage disposal. If she were in Denver she could pick up a doughnut or a bagel or a cinnamon roll or an English muffin on her way to work. Only a cowboy would actually eat oatmeal.

Birdie thanked Luke for the flowers and accepted his flattering words about her baby. When he asked her what she intended to name the baby, she smiled shyly at J.J.

"I thought I'd name her Jacqueline Ann, after you and my grandma. I'll call her Jackie Ann."

Pleasure washed over J.J. at the unexpected compliment. "I'd be honored to have your baby named after me, but..." She hesitated, unsure how to proceed. "What about the baby's father?" she finally asked.

"Some father. The doctor said Ad's knocking me around is probably what caused Jackie Ann to come early." Birdie's face turned red as she tried to keep from crying. "Ad was here this morning. When I told him I wasn't gonna come home on account of his hitting me and maybe hurting the baby, he started yelling at me. The nurse came in and made him leave, but he said he'd take the baby away from me. He said I was too stupid to be a mama."

"He had no business coming to see you. He must have been issued a seventy-two-hour no-contact order," J.J. said.

"My dad picked him up at the jail. He told Ad I had no business airing our dirty laundry in public. Like Jackie Ann's nothing but dirty socks."

"Don't worry, Birdie," Luke said. "Nobody around here is going to let Ad take the baby away from you."

Birdie looked at J.J. "I want a divorce. I know you aren't a lawyer anymore, J.J., now you're Luke's wife and all, but Luke said you were a big lawyer in Denver. You'll get me a divorce, won't you? I can't let Ad hurt Jackie Ann."

J.J. gently touched Birdie's restless hands. "I'm sure there are a number of good lawyers around here. Luke will help you find one."

"I know I don't got the kind of money you must have cost, but I'm gonna get a job and I can send you a little something every month." Birdie picked at her blanket.

"Money has nothing to do with it, Birdie. I don't—"

"I know you don't need money, married to Luke and all."

"Being married to Luke has nothing to do with it. I don't do divorce work."

"You could try and talk Luke into letting you do this one thing, couldn't you? I don't want to cause trouble between you and Luke, honest I don't, but Luke's crazy about you. He'd let you be my lawyer if you wanted to."

J.J. looked at Luke as he stood silently at the foot of the hospital bed. He stared impassively back. J.J. wondered how many other people had heard from Luke she used to be a lawyer in Denver. Birdie's words painted a clear picture of what J.J.'s life would be if she stayed married to Luke. Not that she'd been considering doing such a stupid thing. "I do not need Luke's permission to take a case," J.J. said in a frosty voice.

Birdie's lower lip wobbled. "I guess you only work for important people."

"That's not it. I don't—"

"I know Jackie Ann and I are nobody. I'm not smart like you," Birdie blurted out. "Ad says I'm too stupid to talk to."

"Which shows how dumb he is," J.J. said instantly. "You're not stupid. The stupid one is Ad Parker. He's so dumb he didn't even know how to treat his wife. You and Jackie aren't nobodies. You're somebodies, and don't you ever forget it. You're somebody important." J.J. took a deep breath. "Birdie, you're right about one thing. I only take on important clients. Very important clients. And as of right now, you and Jackie Ann are my clients, and I'll represent your interests to the best of my ability."

Birdie's face glowed. "Thank you." She added solemnly. "I want you to know, J.J., after you helped me birth Jackie Ann, she's like your baby, too."

J.J. thrust aside the unexpected pain. She'd made her choices, and they were the right ones for her. Only fools expected perfect solutions.

As they exited the hospital parking lot, Luke said, "I know what you're thinking, O'Brien, but I did not tell Birdie you were giving up the practice of law or that you were moving here. She asked me where you were from, and I said you were a lawyer in Denver. Any other conclusions she drew came strictly from her own ideas about marriage."

"Do you expect me to believe Birdie's ideas bear no relationship to your ideas about marriage?"

"Listen, lawyer lady, if my thoughts on marriage in any way mirrored Birdie's, I'd have roped and throwed you last year and hauled you back to the ranch and put my brand on you so you knew what pasture you belonged in."

"How provincial. The wife as a husband's possession."

"I used the word 'if.'"

"Admit it. You want a wife who follows you around and does your bidding like a drooling puppy dog."

"My mother has followed my dad around for thirty-five years. There's nothing wrong with wanting a wife who's willing to share my life."

"In other words, give up her own. Move out here to the back of beyond and live with cows."

"You make it sound like a fate worse than death."

"To anybody but a lapdog, it would be," J.J. retorted.

"I don't know why we're having this conversation," Luke said coldly, "since under the circumstances, the kind of wife I'd like doesn't concern you."

"I was merely making idle conversation."

"Sure." They rode in silence until Luke asked, "Why did you refuse at first to take on Birdie as a client? Don't worry about your fee. I'll pay her bills."

"That won't be necessary. The law firm encourages us to take on the occasional pro bono client."

"Will you be stepping on someone else's toes by taking on a divorce case?"

"No."

"Then?"

"Then what?" She knew very well what he wanted to know.

"Why'd you initially turn her down? Oh hell," he slapped the steering wheel. "You didn't want to represent her because you didn't want to come back here."

She grabbed at the excuse he'd handed her. "This isn't exactly a Hawaiian paradise."

Luke shot her a quick look. "Yesterday you thought the snow and mountains beautiful."

"They are. In paintings."

"You're worried about embarrassing me, aren't you? Damn it, O'Brien, I'm a big boy. I'm not going to fall apart if I run into my ex-wife on the street. Nor will I toss you in the snow to make mad, passionate love. Bring Alexander with you."

Heat crawled up J.J.'s face. "This isn't Burton's idea of a vacation hot spot, either."

"You can both stay with me."

"Gee, wouldn't that be peachy keen?"

"I won't even comment at the breakfast table about creaking bedsprings during the night. There's no reason for you to be afraid of taking on Birdie's divorce case."

"I wasn't afraid," J.J. practically shouted. "I don't take divorce cases because I don't like divorce." The minute the angry words left her mouth she could have kicked herself for allowing Luke's ridiculous suppositions to goad her into saying the one statement she would have preferred remained unsaid.

For what seemed an eternity her words echoed in the truck cab over the noise of the engine. Then Luke burst out laughing.

"You can't keep introducing me all over town as your wife when we both know our marriage is about to come to a screeching halt." J.J. flounced with annoyance. As much as one could flounce belted in the front seat of a pickup.

"Would you please let me worry about what my friends will think? I like that blue-green sweater and slacks outfit. You ought to wear that color more often. Matches your eyes."

J.J. ignored both the fashion advice and the strained patience in Luke's voice, which attested to his having already made the first request more than once. "Your friend, the pie-baker—"

"Susan Curtis."

"—communicated quite clearly she thinks I'm lower than the scum of the earth. No doubt all your friends agree with her. Do you enjoy people feeling sorry for you, or are you hoping everyone will snub me and I'll have a miserable time?"

"No one's going to snub you."

"There's assurance I can take to the bank," J.J. said sarcastically. "You're the one who thought the pie baker and I would like each other."

"You would like Susan, if you'd give her a chance."

"I think you've been kicked in the head by a cow."

Luke pulled into a wide circular driveway and stopped behind a number of vehicles already parked there. Dusk had not yet given way to dark, but light streamed through large windows in the long, low, log house hugging the crest of a knoll. Whatever J.J. expected a county sheriff to live in, it wasn't an expensive, modern house like this. Luke opened the passenger door and J.J. stepped down. A dog barked from out back. Wind swirled around her feet bringing the scent of the small junipers that lined the front of the house.

A tall, slender woman with short, curly, chestnut-colored hair answered the door. "Luke!" She threw herself into Luke's embrace before turning to J.J. "You must be J.J. I could hardly wait to meet you." Tossing J.J.'s coat at Luke, the woman grabbed J.J.'s hand and

took her down a long hall to a huge, sunken living room.
"Everyone, say hello to Luke's bride, J. J. O'Brien."
The reddish-haired woman pointed around the room, rattling names off so quickly, J.J. knew she'd never remember a quarter of them. She already knew Susan
Curtis and the sheriff, Everett Bailey, and smiled gratefully as the latter moved to welcome her.

"Margo," the sheriff said, "you forgot somebody."

The woman widened her green eyes. "I don't think
so."

Luke laughed from behind J.J. "Give it up, Ev. Margo
works hard at being a bubblehead. She's convinced mystery writers are supposed to be eccentric. J.J., this is
Margo Bailey."

"My ball and chain," the sheriff said manfully.

"Your reason for living," his wife retorted.

"The albatross around my neck."

"Your personal back-scratcher and foot-warmer."

"Enough!" someone yelled from across the room.
"Don't let them get started, Luke."

Margo sniffed audibly, turned her nose up at all of
them and hustled J.J. out to the kitchen, saying she
needed help. "I don't. That was an excuse so I can grill
you."

"Grill me?" J.J. asked lightly, her heart sinking.

"Ev and Luke have been best friends for eons, so you
have to tell me the worst about you so we can be best
friends." Margo poured two glasses of wine, handed J.J.
one, perched on a tall stool and pointed to a second stool.

J.J. slowly sat and looked around the enormous,
gleaming kitchen. "What a lovely kitchen you have."

"I guess so. Ev and the architect designed it. I don't
cook. Now, tell me everything. All Ev would tell me is
he met you when he went out to arrest Ad Parker." She
scowled. "He wouldn't tell me why he thought that so
darned funny. Ev wouldn't even tell me if you were

beautiful,'' she added indignantly. ''Susan had to tell me that.''

''Susan Curtis?''

Margo nodded her head. ''She said you hated her on sight. She really meant she didn't like you, but that's Susan. She detested me when we met. On account of she thought I treated Ev badly. He was a cop in Denver, and that's why he walks with a limp. Got his leg shot up pretty bad. I'm from Wyoming and when it happened he told me he didn't love me, thinking I shouldn't marry a cripple. Aren't men stupid?''

Understanding the question to be rhetorical, J.J. didn't answer.

''Naturally I told my dad Ev had got me pregnant and Daddy is the police chief, that's how I met Ev, he came to pick up a criminal, so he had to marry me. We hadn't even had sex, but Ev knew there was no point in trying to convince Daddy of that.''

J.J. stared at the other woman in speechless fascination.

Margo went on. ''I can't wait on Ev the way Susan thinks I should because he'll think I feel sorry for him and sometimes I want to cry when his leg hurts so bad, but I joke about it instead, and Susan hates that. Luke probably told you that about five years ago Susan's husband and two little boys were killed by a drunk driver.''

''Oh, no,'' J.J. breathed, shamefully recalling her earlier, ugly taunt that Susan would never be able to make Luke as happy in bed as J.J. had. Of all the horrid things to say to a woman tragically widowed. It probably wasn't even true.

Margo nodded. ''She has a real thing about women who don't appreciate their husbands and children, not that I blame her, but that's no reason to assume every woman falls into that category. She's positive you won't put up with Luke's juvenile delinquents, which makes her as bad as Ev, who was surprised at how levelheaded you were about delivering Birdie Parker's baby. I don't know where their brains are. Luke wouldn't marry a lightweight feather head just because she's beautiful.''

Ignoring Margo's dubious conclusion, J.J. zeroed in on the two words that had caught her immediate attention. "Juvenile delinquents?"

"Luke hasn't told you about Sal and Tony?" Margo shrugged off the subject as unimportant. "He will. Now—" she crossed her long legs and took a sip of wine "—it's your turn to talk."

Trying to decide how to reply, J.J. stared at the mirrored backsplash over the countertops. Wide-set eyes of clear, pale aqua that slanted the barest bit upward gazed back. She liked Margo Bailey too much to lie. Finally she said in a voice deliberately devoid of emotion, "I'm a lawyer from Denver. Luke and I made the mistake of getting married a little over a year ago, and now we're getting divorced."

Absolute silence filled the kitchen. "Well," Margo eventually said in an artificially bright voice, "I asked you to tell me the worst, didn't I?" She hopped down from her stool. "If you'll take this tray of veggies in and set it on the dining-room table, I'll take care of the rest. We're eating buffet style. Please tell Ev he needs to come check his lasagna. I don't have a clue if it's done."

J.J. took the tray. At the kitchen doorway, she turned. "I'm sorry, Margo. I would have liked being your friend."

Margo gave her an astonished look. "Goodness, J.J., just because you and Luke are breaking up, doesn't mean we can't be friends. Although I will have to say—" she frowned darkly "—I thought Luke had better sense than that."

"Than what?"

That's all she needed, J.J. thought. Now Luke would

be justifiably annoyed she'd told Margo about the divorce.

"Luke Remington, it's rude to eavesdrop," Margo scolded. "And you must know eavesdroppers never hear anything good about themselves. You asked, so I'm going to tell you. Ev told me you let Ad Parker get the drop on you with a knife."

"Ev was on his way. I didn't see any point in working up a sweat. Besides, Calamity Jane here galloped to the rescue with her elk antlers."

Margo, not having heard that part of the story, immediately demanded all the details. Her laughter brought the rest of the dinner guests trailing into the kitchen, wanting to know what was so funny. Luke launched into yet another retelling of the episode. The more he told it, the more of an idiot J.J. thought he made her out to be. Clutching the tray of vegetables, she fled the kitchen.

The other guests, ranging from ranchers to storekeepers to schoolteachers, appeared to accept J.J. without reservation. She would have enjoyed the evening had she not been there under false pretenses. No matter how often she told herself legally she was Luke's wife, she knew these people believed her Luke's wife in every sense of the word. Their opinions of her tardy arrival in North Park after marrying Luke a year ago remained their secrets. J.J. was uncomfortably aware they'd view her much differently if they knew J.J. not only planned to divorce Luke, but had already picked out his successor. Whatever Margo Bailey thought of J.J.'s bald announcement of the pending divorce, she kept her thoughts and her knowledge to herself.

Susan Curtis represented the other blot on the evening for J.J. Other than greeting J.J. civilly, Susan made no effort to renew their acquaintance. Having learned of the triple tragedy in Susan's past, J.J. couldn't blame Susan for disliking her. Once, after his wife Caroline had died, Burton had exploded with anger when a young law clerk in the firm had slighted his wife. Susan obviously shared Burton's low opinion of spouses who failed to value their marriage partners.

The Sunday night party broke up early. Luke and J.J. exited the warm luxury of the Baldwin home into a night filled with swirling snowflakes. Burrowing into her down coat, J.J. shivered as she hastened toward the pickup in Luke's wake. "Come on, heater," she said, stamping snow from her feet.

Luke turned the ignition key. "Give the engine a minute to warm up. You survived the party, you can survive a little cold."

"A little cold! In Antarctica the weather gets a little cold. This is freezing. Polar bears couldn't survive here." She didn't want to talk about the party. She hated deceiving people who in other circumstances might have become friends. "It must be fun, knowing a mystery writer."

Luke flipped a blanket from behind the seats over her legs. "Margo drives us nuts. Always looking for a unique way to kill someone. In her last book she used a hay baler. You've probably inspired her to gore a victim to death with elk antlers."

J.J. chose to ignore Luke's teasing remark. "She must make good money writing."

"If you mean the house, the money's from Ev's family. He's a trust fund baby. His parents were high society, always gallivanting around from one beautiful people spot to another. They died in a private plane crash when Ev was ten, leaving him bags of money."

"Margo said he was a policeman in Denver and got shot."

Luke nodded. "Some guy out of his mind on drugs, took his ex-wife and kids hostage. The cops thought they'd convinced him to let the wife and kids go. He said send two cops in for them."

"Oh, no." J.J. anticipated the rest.

"Killed the other cop. They couldn't go in after Ev for fear of endangering the hostages. Didn't matter. The guy killed them all before turning the gun on himself. Ev still thinks he should have been able to save them some way. He quit the force. Might have quit life, but Margo wouldn't let him. It may be noble to release a woman from an engagement because you're crippled. It's not too noble to ditch her when she's pregnant."

"I thought Ev knew Margo wasn't pregnant."

"He knew it. Everett Jr. came along nine months and two days after the wedding. Ev said he didn't want people calling his wife a liar."

"Using pregnancy to force a man into marriage seems manipulative and potentially damaging to the marriage."

"Margo likes to play at being eccentric, but she has a wise head on her shoulders. She knew she and Ev belonged together."

"They seem so different."

"As night and day," Luke agreed, "but they complement each other, bring out the best in each other. Like yin and yang, peanut butter and jelly."

Not a subject J.J. wished to pursue. "How in the world did a rich kid grow up to be a policeman?"

"After his folks died, Ev's relatives didn't want to bother with him. He embarked on a life of petty crime, demonstrating he didn't give a damn about them, either. At age eighteen his guardian gave him a choice between the army or prison. Ev chose the army, did his stint, got out, went to college and joined the Denver police force. He figured his youthful life of crime prepared him for understanding other criminals."

"Why are they living in North Park?"

"Ev stayed at the ranch while recuperating. The sheriff's job here opened up about the time he and Margo got married. Ev didn't want to go back to Denver, and although he could have lived off his investment income, he didn't feel that was the best way to bring up a kid."

"Did you meet your juvenile delinquents through Ev?"

"Who told you about Tony and Sal? Margo, I suppose. Discount at least half what she says. She never can resist improving on the truth if it's boring. If the fellows were hardened criminals and murderers, Margo wouldn't be inviting them to join her family's activities every summer."

"She didn't tell me any such thing. In fact, she didn't tell me anything. She said you'd tell me."

The wind flung icy crystals against the windshield faster than the wipers could handle the onslaught. "I suppose I should, in case you hear false rumors in town." Luke squinted into the darkness. "Sal's brother involved him in the robberies of three convenience stores and a gas station. A pimp got Tony's older sister addicted to heroine, and she died of an overdose. Tony put the pimp in the hospital. Sal was fifteen, and Tony sixteen. Ev knew they were good kids who just needed a chance, so he worked out something with the courts, and I took them here, four, five years ago. Summers and holidays." Luke laughed. "I worked their behinds off."

"Was Ev right about them?" J.J. asked doubtfully.

"Who they were isn't as important as who they are today. Tony's as smart as they come. He made the Dean's list at the University of Colorado last semester. Sal's in prelaw there. He'll make a good lawyer."

J.J. didn't bother to ask who was paying the young men's tuitions. "Bad boys gone good. You and Ev and your delinquents. Is that why you took them on? No," she answered her own question. "Because of your uncle Zane. You told me you got into trouble in high school and your folks sent you to stay with him."

Luke shrugged. "I never got around to thanking him."

J.J. studied Luke's rugged profile. The darkness concealed the cleft in his chin. She didn't practice criminal law, but she'd been around courthouses enough to know a person didn't turn around a young man's life just by hiring him to baby-sit cows. It took dedication, discipline and a helping hand. More important, someone had to care.

Luke cared. A person would have to be dead to miss the caring, affection and satisfaction in Luke's voice. He sounded like a proud father.

One day Luke would remarry and have children who'd climb all over the huge Belgian draft horses and tumble off hay bales as they fed the cattle with their father. They'd have snowball fights with their father. Learn to ride ponies at their father's side. J.J. could picture the children, hazel-eyed sons and daughters.

She turned her head and looked out her window. The horizontally blowing snow curtained off the outside of the truck from the outside world. An enormous lump obstructed her throat, and she couldn't prevent herself from touching the beauty mark by her mouth. She wouldn't have to worry about passing the hated full bottom lip or detestable beauty mark on to a daughter or granddaughter. Oddly the knowledge gave her zero comfort.

CHAPTER SEVEN

THE heater pumped warmth into the pickup cab as icy pellets pinged monotonously off the outside of the truck like miniature BBs. The windshield wipers snicked back and forth. J.J. peered into the maelstrom of snowflakes, hypnotized by their wild dance in the headlight beams.

"Hey, slow down, you crazy fool!" Luke yelled, before swearing viciously.

Startled from her drowsy state, J.J. snapped to attention as a large, dark shape materialized from behind, its headlights sweeping up to run beside them. Luke swore again as the other vehicle bumped Luke's side of the pickup. The pickup lurched and swerved as Luke fought to keep it on the road. The other vehicle, a truck larger than Luke's, nudged them again. Cursing fluently Luke battled grimly, as the other truck toyed with them, speeding up or slowing down to match Luke's speed, then randomly bumping them.

They approached a curve in the road, and the tension flowing from Luke jacked up a notch. The whine of the engine beside them intensified, and the dark shape roared up and squarely rammed the front of Luke's pickup. The pickup left the roadbed, bumping and jolting its way across the ground, stopping abruptly with a loud screeching noise.

"You okay?" Luke switched off the engine.

"Yes, I think so. You?"

"Stay here. That crazy son of—" Luke disappeared into the storm, slamming the truck door behind him.

J.J. slumped against the back of the seat. Luke had left on the headlights, which illuminated thin willow branches bowing in the wind. The side windows framed a wall of blowing snow. The faint sound of a car horn penetrated the storm.

Luke climbed back into the truck bringing a blast of arctic air with him. He brushed snow off his head and shoulders and gave J.J. a piercing look. "Sure you're okay?"

"Yes. What was that all about?"

"That damned fool Parker, playing games. Probably drunker 'n a skunk. He had the gall to honk and wave as he drove back to town."

"Maybe he'll tell someone what happened."

Luke snorted angrily. "Don't bet on it." Turning the key in the ignition, he alternately begged and swore at the pickup as he spent the next few minutes futilely attempting to rock the vehicle from its icy resting place. With one final curse, he shut off the engine.

The silence was deafening. "What do we do now? Walk?"

"What the hell do you think we do?" He switched off the headlights, encasing them in a world of swirling snow. The wind howled around the truck, beating it with willow whips and shaking it in fury. "We wait."

"Wait for what?" Luke's solution left a lot to be desired. "There must be something you—we can do."

"In case you haven't looked outside, O'Brien, it's snowing."

"We have snow in Denver. I recognize it when I see it."

"Do you also recognize we're two miles from home?"

"Two miles," she said with relief. "I can walk two miles."

"Sure you can. In a city park on a nice spring day. You'd be whining about the cold and the snow before we covered half a mile. That's two miles as the crow flies. Another two miles longer by the road."

"Then we'll have to be crows."

"In this storm, if we left the road, we'd be lost before we walked twenty yards."

"I am not going to spend the night in the truck."

"How's that?" Luke shifted his large frame beneath her.

"Really, really uncomfortable. I don't know why they put stupid gearshifts there." J.J. tried to fit herself to the narrow bench seat and Luke's semireclining body. At least she couldn't complain of being cold. Living in blizzard country, Luke traveled prepared. Which is why they were currently packed inside a sleeping bag as if they were two sardines. Inside the zippered bag, Luke had unfolded a reflective emergency blanket over her, and the heavy wool blanket she'd had on her lap now covered the sleeping bag, Luke and J.J. She wore a stocking hat Luke had dug out from under the seat. He'd put their shoes on the floor, and their coats lay across their feet. Beneath her, Luke was a raging furnace. Her pulse began to accelerate.

"Damn it, O'Brien, will you quit wiggling?"

"I can't get comfortable. You're too bumpy."

"I wouldn't be so bumpy if you'd quit wiggling." He laughed softly at her sudden rigidity. "On the other hand, I might be able to find someplace to put one of those bumps."

"Just my luck to be snowbound with a silver-tongued devil," J.J. said sarcastically. "I couldn't help myself, Ma," she trilled in a false voice, "his purty words swept me off my feet."

"They stopped your wiggling."

"I still don't see why we can't do something to get us out of this mess instead of spending the night in the truck."

"Sometimes the best plan of attack is patiently waiting to see what's going to happen before you make your move."

"You must be president of the procrastinators' club."

"Didn't your mother ever tell you patience is a virtue?"

"She told me to fight for what I wanted," J.J. said.

"The two aren't mutually exclusive."

Since she couldn't figure out how to refute that, J.J. said nothing. For the next few minutes the only sounds were the storm battering against the truck and the truck rattling in defiance. And the beat of Luke's heart beneath her ear. The back of J.J.'s leg itched and her foot threatened to cramp. She didn't dare move. Luke's breath warmed her face, and his legs twined through hers. His hard thighs supported her. Their arms encircled each other in a loverlike embrace. If she turned her head and unbuttoned his shirt, she could paint his chest with kisses.

She wondered if it was possible to make love in a sleeping bag. What a dumb thought. The brutal cold necessitated their present position. Any tension emanating from Luke's body was strictly a product of her imagination. If he and one of his cowhands had been stranded under similar circumstances, the two men would wisely huddle together to defeat the cold. J.J. had lived in Colorado long enough to know all about the hazards of hypothermia. She couldn't remember if the niggling craving deep inside her was one of the symptoms. Think of something else, she told herself. Sublimate. "I'm hungry."

"You just ate," Luke said.

"When it's this cold, a body needs fuel for warmth. Don't you have candy bars or something we can gnaw on?"

"If we're still here tomorrow night, you can have one."

"Tomorrow night! I'm not staying here past morning if I have to chop down those willows and make myself snowshoes."

His chest shook with silent laughter. "J. J. O'Brien, intrepid mountain woman." He shifted, rearranging her across his sprawling body.

J.J. jammed her fingers into the sleeping bag behind Luke's back. His every move tantalized and tormented body parts sensitized by their enforced intimacy. He stretched beneath her, brushing his chest against her swelling breasts in a move as potent as a lover's caress. "You know what you said about me wiggling?" she asked tightly. "Your wiggling doesn't exactly put me to sleep. If you don't stop moving around, we'll be finding out just how easy it is for two people to have sex in a sleeping bag designed for one."

Her words hung in the frigid air. If she could have moved, J.J. would have kicked herself. Because she was aroused by their situation didn't mean Luke felt the same. She'd shocked him speechless. "Never mind," she muttered. "It's just I'm incredibly uncomfortable. You're taking up way too much room, I think my back is about to break in half and I'm hungry." Desire jolted her body as Luke changed position, his thigh coming to rest between her legs. Blood drummed in her ears. Closing her eyes, J.J. forced herself to lie perfectly still and breathe slowly. When she felt she had control of her vocal chords, she said, "If you don't move that leg away from there immediately, I'm going to seriously injure you."

Luke carefully moved his leg. "I know this is awkward, but it's crucial we keep warm in weather like this. I'm not going to jump your bones."

"I know that."

"Unless you want me to," he said in a neutral voice.

J.J.'s throat muscles froze. She couldn't answer because the truth was, she did want to make love with Luke. And she didn't. She couldn't make love with the man she intended to divorce. Once, in a weak moment such as the other night was one thing, but to make love again... No matter how much her body ached to become one with his. Physical gratification for purely selfish reasons was wrong, not to mention the unfairness of using Luke again. "I don't want to want you to," she finally said.

After an eternity, Luke said, "I'm going to unzip the sleeping bag enough to reach under my seat and grab a couple of candy bars." He suited actions to words.

Giving J.J. time to think. "I knew if I went about it the right way, I could weasel food out of you." She took the candy bar he held out to her, quickly tearing open the wrapper.

"Risky business, playing those kinds of games." Luke unwrapped his candy, took a bite and chewed slowly. "I might have interpreted your ambivalent answer to mean you wanted me to seduce you into making love." He took another bite. "We both know I could have."

The candy lost its appeal. J.J. carefully folded the wrapper over the half-eaten bar and set it on the dashboard. "I'll save this for breakfast tomorrow. Now I think I'll try to sleep."

Closing her eyes, she listened to the wind and the snow and Luke's heartbeat and the sound of his chewing. Luke must be elated at how well her visit to his ranch was turning out. A little over a week had passed, and already his passion for her had cooled off.

If only blizzards and subzero temperatures could cool down the physical attraction Luke held for her.

Paper crumpled near her ear and dropped to the floor with a faint sound. Luke shifted, gave an exasperated groan, shifted again, tightened his arms around J.J. and finally lay still. His deep, rhythmic breathing lulled her into restless sleep.

J.J. woke suddenly. False dawn lightened the sky, but the raging storm kept visibility almost nil. Cold nipped at her nose, but the rest of her stayed toasty warm. Taking advantage of Luke's deep sleep, she snuggled against him, deriving guilty pleasure from the feel of his firm, masculine body against her.

Long-suppressed memories escaped from their hiding place to replay in her mind the idyllic week she and Luke had shared in the days from meeting to parting. The ending she shied away from, concentrating instead on the tenderness, the exhilaration. She'd loved the way he filled his faded jeans. He'd loved her classic, pastel silk underwear. He'd laughed at her when she said buttered popcorn was fattening and insisted on hand-feeding her popped kernels yellow with butter. She'd licked the residue from his fingers.

She'd stood in front of him wearing a pale aqua silk teddy and repeated the arguments she'd made in court that day. The arguments that had won her case. He'd saluted her with his coffee mug and made love to her on the rich rose Chinese throw rug in front of her gas fireplace.

J.J. tried to transfer the scene to Luke's living room with its worn beige wall-to-wall carpet and cowhide rug in front of a huge stone fireplace. Her imagination wasn't that good.

A sound from outside the pickup broke through her reverie, and J.J. realized she'd heard the sound earlier. Someone was stomping through the snow. Her breath caught. Adrian Parker. Then common sense took over, and she knew someone passing had seen the truck through the snow and was coming to investigate. "Luke," she whispered. "Wake up."

Hazel eyes blinked open and regarded her solemnly. Luke's mouth slowly curved. "You have a chocolate beauty mark matching the one on the other side your great-whatever-grandmother gave you." Before J.J. could free her arm from the sleeping bag to wipe her face, Luke bent his head and licked the speck of chocolate. "Cold skin," he murmured.

Warm tongue, she almost said, catching herself in the nick of time. Her mouth close to Luke's face, she said quietly, "Someone is coming. Shouldn't we get out of the sleeping bag?"

Luke tensed and looked over her shoulder, peering sharply into the driving snow. Then he relaxed and chuckled softly. "Move slowly and quietly so you can see out the window on the passenger side. Quiet, now. We don't want to spook her."

"Her?" J.J. managed to shift her upper body, only once digging her elbows into Luke's chest, until she could see out the window as directed. She saw nothing but snow.

"Give it a second," Luke said in her ear. "Every once in a while the wind shifts direction, and there's a little break in the snow. There. See her?"

Visible through a curtain of snow stood a large, dark ungainly looking animal. "She's a moose, isn't she? A real live moose, right outside the window. Look," J.J. half whispered, "there's another one." The two animals made their way through the deep snow, their long legs moving majestically.

"A cow and her calf from last summer."

J.J. held her breath until the two large animals moved away, then she emptied her lungs all at once and flopped down on Luke's chest. "Why do you suppose they were here? Curiosity about what we're doing?"

"Moose feed on willows, and we happen to be parked right in the middle of a willow-lined creek."

They lay quietly as the sky took on a lighter cast. Finally Luke reached over and unzipped the sleeping bag. "Pleasant as this is, it's not getting us home. No, you stay here in the sleeping bag," he said as J.J. scrambled to get out.

"I'm coming with you."

"No, you're not." He extracted his long legs from the sleeping bag and quickly zipped up the bag before J.J. could react.

"Give me one good reason why I can't. And don't you dare say it's because I'm a woman."

"I'll give you two good reasons. Your shoes."

As much as she wanted to argue, J.J. admitted Luke had a point. Her sensible loafers were designed for mall-crawling, not for hiking cross-country in snow above her knees.

Luke reached behind the seat and pulled out a pair of mud-encrusted boots and tugged them on. Next he dredged up a black ski mask and fur-lined leather gloves. Shrugging into his sheepskin jacket, he looked at J.J.. "I don't know how long it will take me to reach the ranch. I'll follow the fence line. With luck, the moose will be gone so I won't have to detour around them. Cow moose are notoriously bad-tempered when they have a youngster around. If she comes back, watch her, but don't talk to her or make any moves toward her. If she gets riled, she'll take on the pickup. And the pickup might lose."

"I won't rile the moose."

"There are a couple of energy bars under the seat." He grabbed one and stuck it into his pocket.

"Check."

He captured her chin with his gloved hand. "Now this is an order."

"I don't take orders—"

"You'll take this one." He shook her chin for emphasis. "Do not, under any circumstances, leave the truck. If you even think about starting after me..." His fingers tightened. "You don't know the country. You aren't dressed for being out in a blizzard. You wouldn't last thirty minutes. You are to stay right here. Do you understand."

"I'm not completely stupid. I—"

"I want your solemn promise you won't leave the

truck and start walking.'' He shook her chin a little harder. ''Promise!''

''Oh, honestly, all right, I promise,'' she said in a disgruntled voice. ''I wish you'd give me credit for having at least half a brain.''

Luke's grasp of her chin eased. ''I give you credit for having two halves of a brain, but I don't always approve of the use to which you put them.''

''I wouldn't want to do anything a man disapproves of, would I?''

''Don't turn this into a stupid man-woman contest, O'Brien. I'm not dumb enough to say I'm ordering you to stay put for your own good. I'm ordering you to stay here so I don't have to explain to Alexander why I allowed you to freeze to death.''

''You don't have to belabor the obvious. I said I'd stay.''

''You promised you'd stay,'' he reminded her.

''Okay, I promised.''

He covered her cheeks with his gloved palms. ''I could be gone only a couple of hours, could be most of the day. I don't know how tough the going will be.'' The ski mask, which covered all but his mouth and eyes, turned him into a sinister stranger. Until J.J. saw his eyes. Hazel eyes, which focused intensely on J.J., as if memorizing every pore of her skin. ''I know waiting won't be easy, but no one's going to be out on this side road during a blizzard, and no one will be looking for us. Jeff and Dale will assume we stayed in town, and Ev will think we made it home. I'd rather not leave you, but I don't have much choice.''

''Would you be this concerned about leaving me if I were a man? I'll be fine.''

''I know you will, and I'll be back for you, so stay here.''

''If you order me to stay one more—''

Luke took possession of her mouth. The frigid air had

chilled his lips, but his kiss warmed her to the bottoms of her stockinged feet. He straightened up. "Okay, O'Brien, stay—"

"Don't you dare say it!"

He grinned, a lopsided grin framed by the mouth opening of the ski mask. "Stay bundled up." Arctic air rushed in as he stepped outside, battling the wind as it grabbed for the door.

"Luke!" J.J. scrambled to reach the door before he shut it. When he turned, she struggled to find the right words. "Being snowbound with you wasn't so bad," she finally said. The wind caught her words and flung them into the blizzard.

Luke cupped his wrapped ear with his hand. "What?"

"Be careful," she shouted, exaggerating the shape of her mouth so if he didn't hear, he could at least read her lips.

Luke nodded and slammed the door shut.

The snow that had entered with his departure drifted slowly downward to land softly on the blanket. Gently J.J. picked up a snowflake with the tip of her gloved finger. The six-pointed star glittered in the half light of the storm. So perfect, so beautiful. The stellar crystal melted into a tiny damp spot on J.J.'s glove. So short-lived. Snowflakes, like marriages, needed the right conditions to survive.

Snuggled deep in the sleeping bag, little besides her nose peeking out, J.J. had long ago concluded Luke had decided she wasn't worth returning for. She'd read people could survive almost anything as long as they had water. She had plenty of that. She wasn't as warm without Luke's body heat, but she didn't think she'd freeze to death. No, a skilled coroner would determine her death had been caused by a caffeine deficiency. She'd do anything for a cup of coffee.

She heard the horses first. The jangling sounds of harness roused her from her self-pity, and she struggled to sit up. She was still fighting with a recalcitrant sleeping bag zipper when Luke pounded on the locked door. Scooting along the seat, she managed to reach the lock.

Snow and polar air blew into the truck as Luke stuck in his upper body. Snow coated his head and shoulders. Tiny clumps of ice clung to his eyelashes. "Think I'd forgotten you?"

She'd never seriously doubted he'd return. "You stopped to eat breakfast, didn't you?"

"Bacon and eggs, hash browns, waffles, pancakes, toast," Luke teased in an obvious lie. Seeing J.J.'s battle with the zipper, he reached over and worked it down. "Put your coat on, and I'll zip you back inside."

"I'm not going to wear a sleeping bag." She slid her arms into her coat.

"Sure you are. It's the latest style." Before she could argue further, he yanked the zipper up to her neck, effectively binding her arms to her sides.

"Undo this zip—" She spit out fabric as Luke pulled a knit balaclava over her head.

He adjusted it so she could see, then added the lined cap with ear flaps. "Ready?"

"Ready for what?" The balaclava muffled her words.

Her answer came as Luke pulled her from the truck into the storm. Holding her close to his chest, he bumped the truck door shut with his shoulder, then labored through the deep snow to the hay sled. Icy crystals beat painfully against the exposed part of J.J.'s face, forcibly demonstrating what Luke had endured on his long trek back to the ranch.

Johnny and Hondo stood patiently in front of the sled. Clouds of vapor poured from their nostrils and snow covered their bodies. Small icicles hung from their noses.

Luke put J.J. down behind a row of hay bales stacked

four feet high at the front of the sled, then set bales on either side of her in a kind of cocoon sheltering her from the worst of the storm. He jumped from the sled and disappeared in the direction of the truck. Returning in minutes, he dropped a plastic bag beside her. "Your shoes and purse," he shouted.

The wind stole J.J.'s shouted thanks.

With a grin and with a flourish, Luke pulled a sack from out of the baled hay. He squatted down beside J.J. and took an insulated cup from the sack.

The fragrant smell of coffee mingled with the steam pouring from the drinking hole in the lid. "Coffee," J.J. said gratefully. She couldn't get her arms out of the sleeping bag.

Luke took a sip of the steaming beverage. "What will you give me for it?" he teased in a voice loud enough to be heard over the storm.

"Anything," she shouted.

Unzipping the sleeping bag enough to allow J.J. to free her arms, he wrapped her gloved hands around the mug.

J.J. closed her eyes and breathed deeply of the fragrant aroma. She pulled the balaclava down below her mouth. The coffee warmed and soothed and satisfied all the way down. She opened her eyes. Luke's face was inches from hers. His lips moved, but the wind and the snow stole the sound of his words. No smile curved his mouth. The teasing light had disappeared from his eyes. Standing, he gathered up the reins and shouted at the horses. The sled lurched into motion.

J.J. took another sip of coffee. She might not have heard Luke's response, but she'd had no trouble reading his lips. After she'd told him, "Anything," he'd said, "I might hold you to that." As the horses struggled through the snow, J.J. shivered, though the sleeping bag and the shelter of hay bales kept her warm enough. "Anything" covered a lot of territory. Reason told her he'd been joking. She swallowed more coffee and wondered what she'd do if Luke tried to collect by ordering her into his bed.

CHAPTER EIGHT

YESTERDAY'S storm seemed a distant memory, the sun warming the air while huge puffy clouds sailed serenely across a sapphire sky. J.J. could hardly believe that less than twenty-four hours ago she'd huddled in a sleeping bag while the huge draft horses had fought their way through the tail end of the blizzard to haul her and Luke back to his ranch house. She wished she were back on the sled now.

Luke reined in his horse. "There's something you don't see in Denver."

J.J. followed the direction of his gaze. Two enormous brown birds took off from the ground and spiraled aloft. Rabbit tracks dotted the pasture land beneath the horses' hooves, and J.J. avoided looking at the furred object the birds abandoned on the snow. "What kind of hawks are they?" she asked, shifting uncomfortably in her saddle.

"They're golden eagles. Probably wintering here."

J.J. studied the birds with renewed interest, noting their large heads, lighter brown than their bodies, and their menacing hooked beaks. One eagle returned to the ground, hunching protectively over his meal as he tore at it. The other flew off. J.J. watched until he disappeared in the distance. The second bird soon finished and lifted into the sky to vanish.

With the birds' departure, J.J.'s thoughts returned to her aching muscles. "I told you I'd never ridden a horse. You could have given me one I didn't have to do the splits to ride." Standing gingerly in the stirrups, she rubbed her bottom. "This has got to be the fattest, most inappropriately named horse I've ever seen. No offense,

Fawn—'' she patted the shaggy mare's neck ''—but I'll be crippled for life.'' Fawn snorted a cloud of vapor into the air.

Luke laughed. "C'mon, greenhorn, we still have missing cattle to look for. If any fence came down in the storm, the cows could have drifted down the valley.''

"We weren't all born on horses, you know,'' J.J. groused, bouncing along like a sack of grain, slipping and sliding all over the saddle. Resentfully she eyed Luke's loose, easy way of riding. "I thought pickups had replaced horses.''

"As you should know by now, pickups run better on plowed roads than in unplowed pastures.''

After calling the sheriff to report the accident and Adrian Parker's part in it, Luke had used the tractor to pull the pickup from the creek. Which raised another point. "Your employees use the tractor to feed these cows. They don't have to ride horses.''

"Jeff said when he fed this morning the count was short. Using the tractor to ride the fence line is expensive and inefficient.'' Luke nodded toward a small nearby rise of ground. "I'm going up there to look around.''

The wind had drifted the snow in this area leaving patches of ground covered with only an inch or so of snow. Luke urged his reddish horse, Durango, into a ground-covering gait. They didn't so much trot as flow up the hill. On top Luke sat silhouetted against the sky, raised up in his saddle, looking in all directions. Master of all he surveyed, J.J. thought, in his sheepskin jacket and cowboy hat tipped low over his forehead. He didn't look like a man who'd be happy trapped in traffic jams on Denver's thoroughfares. Like the eagles, Luke needed room in which to soar.

The snow sparkled and crunched beneath Fawn's trudging feet. J.J. winced and shifted her smarting bottom, searching in vain for a more comfortable position. From the top of the rise, Luke waved to her, signaling her to join him. She tapped Fawn's side with her heel, then desperately hung on to the saddle horn as the mare jogged up the rise. Every time one of Fawn's hooves hit the ground, pain jolted through J.J.'s body. She and Fawn definitely did not flow up the hill.

"How you doing, tenderfoot?"

"My feet aren't what's tender." Luke's aviator sunglasses reflected twin images of herself. A knit band covered her ears under the felt wide-brimmed hat Luke had plonked on her head. In spite of the sunscreen he'd insisted she slather on her face, she could almost see her nose turning red. She couldn't see Luke's eyes, but she sensed him staring at her. "What are you looking at? My nose is sunburned, isn't it?"

"It's a little pink. Looks kinda cute." At the grimace she gave him, he said, "Look around. Take your mind off your troubles."

"It's not troubles my mind is on."

Luke grinned, but wisely refrained from comment. Instead he pointed out the Park Range to the west, the Medicine Bow Range to the east, the Never Summer Range to the southeast and the Rabbit Ears Range to the south. "North Park is a intermountain glacial basin. The headwaters of the North Platte River are here, and the tributaries and creeks running into the Platte attracted people to this valley. The Ute Indians hunted here in the summer. Miners and trappers came looking for gold and furs. Explorers, including John Fremont, wandered through, but it took farmers and ranchers in the late 1800s to homestead and settle the valley."

"Including your Stirling ancestors."

He nodded. "A number of ranches around here are owned by families who go back to those early settlers. Families who worked hard to keep their ranches going, at times in the face of incredible odds—the depression, the vagaries of the market, the weather." Luke looked around. "All this is their reward."

"All what? Sunburn, frostbite and sore bottoms? I'll bet there were Stirlings who could hardly wait to escape to a job in the city. For most of us, heated office buildings win out over feeding cows in blizzards any day."

"I've never understood that. I couldn't leave the land. Ranching isn't a job—it's a way of life. You work hard, sleep sound, breathe fresh air." He gazed into the distance, his hands resting on the saddle horn. "A man has room to stretch. There's not a hell of a lot of glamour to this life, but I'm my own man out here. It suits me," he added simply.

He'd be his own man wherever he was, whatever he did. And judging by what she'd seen so far, there wasn't much Luke couldn't do. Cowhand, horse trainer, fence mender, businessman, mechanic, construction worker, odd jobs worker. Lover.

Fawn moved unexpectedly as J.J. involuntarily squeezed the mare between her legs. J.J. clutched the saddle horn and centered herself back in the saddle, replacing her foot in a lost stirrup. And resolved to pay more attention to what she was doing and less to what she wasn't doing.

"Damn," Luke said.

"It's not my fault she has St. Vitus' dance."

Luke looked at the placid dun-colored mare and then at J.J. "What are you talking about?"

"Never mind. What are you talking about?"

"Look down there. Snow drifted up and over the fence and the wind packed it down. Those cows have walked right over it. We'll have to move this whole group to the next pasture."

"Why can't you feed them over there?"

"That's not our land. If we don't move those cows, the whole herd will find its way over there."

"Why don't they come back the way they went?"

"My guess is they can't. The other side of the drift slopes south. The sun came out yesterday once the snow stopped, and the surface of the drift on that side probably melted, then froze during the night. I'll bet that slope is slicker 'n greased lightning. Cows going over the fence this morning could have met with real trouble. We'll need to check for broken legs and sprained knees." Luke headed his horse toward a large white metal gate in the fence. "Let's move 'em out."

"No way." J.J. followed him through the opened gate. "I'm not breaking my neck rounding up any cows."

"I'll swing out and gather any strays. Fawn's no cow pony. All you have to do is get behind the cattle and ride slowly, moving them toward the gate. You won't have any trouble." Grinning at the skeptical look on her face, he headed for a small willow-lined gully, quickly disappearing from sight.

J.J. leaned on the saddle horn, levering her sore bottom out of the saddle. She looked at the half-dozen cows this side of the fence. The cows stared impassively back. They had no intention of going through that gate. She knew it and they knew it. If they could talk they'd be taunting her, "Betcha can't make us. Betcha can't, betcha can't." J.J. could almost see her younger brothers' faces imprinted on the cows. "Just watch me," she shouted.

Fawn snorted in alarm, gave a little jump and J.J. catapulted through the air. She landed flat on her back atop crusted snow as soft as concrete. The fall knocked the air from her, and she doubled up in pain until she could breathe again. Regaining her breath occurred simultaneously with the realization she was on the ground in the middle of a herd of cows. Cautiously she opened her eyes and raised her head to look around. The last of the cows trotted docilely through the open gate. Fawn, one rein dragging on the snow, ambled behind them.

J.J. flopped back to the ground. As mattresses go, the packed snow was hard and cold. For comfort it was a million times better than riding Fawn. J.J. shut her eyes. From the other side of the fence came the sounds of mooing cattle. She heard the snow collapsing beneath their enormous hooves. Fawn nickered quizzically, no doubt wondering at the peculiar behavior of her erstwhile rider.

Let her wonder. J.J. thought she might never move again.

Gradually an odd sensation of being watched prickled the back of J.J.'s neck. Cold snow, she tried to convince herself, but the eerie feeling persisted. She opened her eyes. And immediately wished she hadn't. Five cows ringed her, puzzlement writ large on their bovine faces. Disgusting drool dripped from noses and mouths. J.J. slammed her eyelids down. Play dead, she told herself. Surely that's what they always advise when you're attacked by wild animals. Her muscles locked in dreaded anticipation of tons of cow trampling her body.

Around her the snow snapped and crackled. The next sound would be that of her head popping. One cow, then another mooed. J.J.'s pulse raced with fear. Blood thudded against her eardrums. Something touched her chest then savagely ripped at her down ski parka. J.J. let out a blood-curdling scream.

"What the hell?"

Her eyes popped open. Luke's face hovered over her. He'd discarded his hat, and his dark brown hair looked black in the glaring sunlight, the undisciplined wave hanging down over his forehead. His dark eyebrows met in a heavy frown above eyes J.J. would have sworn were filled with fear before he blinked all emotion from them. Nostrils flared at the end of his well-shaped nose, and his lips thinned. She'd always admired his strong jaw. A jaw that now appeared to be hewn from stone.

J.J. forgot her fall, the cows, her aching muscles, her cold bed. Reaching up with a gloved finger, she traced the shadowy cleft in his chin. "Do you have any idea how sexy this is?"

A muscle jerked in his jaw. "Do you have any idea how much you scared me?"

She ran her finger along his bottom lip and considered his reaction if she pulled his head down within range of her mouth. "Why did I scare you?" she asked absently.

Luke's frown deepened. "Are you all right? Did you hit your head when you fell?"

J.J. gave a little laugh. "I hit everything." She smoothed the deep V between his eyes. "If you don't quit frowning, you'll get horrible wrinkles."

He grabbed her fingers, squeezing them painfully. "What happened?"

She lifted her other hand and ran her fingers over his jawline. The jerking muscle fascinated her. He'd asked her something. "What happened?" she repeated in a vague voice before giving him a slow, seductive smile. "Nothing yet. How long does a gal have to wait before a cowboy gets around to kissing her?"

Luke froze, his narrowed gaze skimming over her face. "Oh hell," he said and lowered his head, slanting his mouth unceremoniously over hers.

His lips were hard and cold. They sent a river of liquid heat through J.J.'s veins. Heat that spread and intensified as Luke blanketed her body with his. Holding her face between his gloved hands, he thrust his tongue between her lips and took possession of her mouth. J.J. wrapped her arms around his middle, fitting their bodies together as their tongues engaged in a fierce mating dance. Their legs tangled, one of Luke's dividing her thighs. His nose was cold, his mouth moist and hot. She hugged him tighter, trying to crawl into his skin. A thin cracking noise split the air.

Luke broke off the kiss. "Damn it, O'Brien, what the hell are you doing laying on the ground? When I saw you I thought—'' He stopped short, pressing his lips tightly together.

"Thought what?" she asked inattentively, admiring his cleft chin. If she lifted her head the tiniest little bit, she could explore it with her tongue. There was something erotic about whisker stubble rasping against the tip of her tongue.

Before she could act on the thought, Luke unlocked her hands from behind him and sat up. He pulled a pair of sunglasses from the breast pocket of his heavy jacket. The bridge of the glasses had snapped in two. He dangled the two pieces over her nose.

J.J. shrugged. "Sue me."

"Sue you. I ought to—" He clamped his mouth shut and sprang abruptly to his feet.

J.J.'s gaze leisurely traveled over Luke's worn boots and up his long, denim-covered legs.

"I'm going to ask you one more time." Ramming the broken glasses back into his pocket, he planted his fists on his hips and glared down at J.J.. "What happened? Are you okay?"

The anger in his voice captured J.J.'s full attention. Luke Remington was absolutely furious. Cautiously she raised her head and looked around. The cows no longer stood around her. "What happened to the cows?"

"They scattered when I charged over here."

The tail end of the only cow in sight in this pasture disappeared back into the willows. No wonder Luke was well on his way to throwing a temper tantrum. "I'm sorry," she said in chagrin. "Now you have to go find them again."

"Forget the cows. Are you okay?"

"Yes." Slowly, judiciously testing each move, she pulled herself into a sitting position.

Luke held out a hand to assist her. "You sure?"

J.J. carefully stood. Every muscle in her body

screamed at her. She rubbed her bottom. "If I never ride another horse the rest of my life, I'll die happy."

"Do you mean to tell me you got off Fawn and were laying on the ground because of a few sore muscles?" He picked up her hat and crammed it back on her head.

From the tone of his voice, he would have preferred she'd at least have been knocked off the horse by a grizzly bear and run over by a herd of buffalo. "I did not get off," J.J. said indignantly. "That stupid horse bucked me off."

"Fawn threw you?" Luke repeated incredulously. "Impossible. She can't work up that much energy." Putting two fingers between his lips, he gave a sharp whistle. Fawn looked at him, then shuffled lethargically in their direction. Luke grabbed the mare's reins and turned toward J.J. "Well?"

"You can 'well?' me till the cows come home, which judging by their disappearance may be sometime next summer, but I am not getting on that darned horse again."

Luke raised an eyebrow.

"Don't give me that arrogant look. I'll walk first."

Luke's lips twitched. "I don't think so."

J.J. didn't like his smile. She backed slowly away from him. He didn't move, just watched her, a look of unrestrained amusement on his face. She was about to ask him what was so darned funny when she smacked into something big and solid. The low bellow in her ear sent J.J. flying across the pasture. She didn't even argue when Luke tossed her into the saddle. She had entirely too much pride to comment on the fact his shoulders shook with laughter.

Durango had wandered up when Luke whistled for Fawn, and Luke swung into his saddle. Man and horse guided through the open gate the cow who'd ambushed J.J. "You and Fawn sit here in front of the gate so these cows—" he pointed to his pasture "—don't get any fancy ideas. I'll gather the others and haze 'em up this way. Move out of the way when you see them coming.'' He crowded Fawn toward the gate with his horse, then grabbed J.J.'s saddle horn, leaned over and planted a hard kiss on her mouth. "And, O'Brien, if Fawn turns into a bucking bronc again, stay on. Next time I'll send you after those damned cows.'' He trotted toward the gully, swooping low to snatch his hat off the snow.

J.J. refused to be impressed. Not even when Luke reappeared shortly trailing four cows. He herded them into his own pasture and closed the gate.

On the other side of the pasture, the large ranch tractor circled a field, distributing hay. The cows saw and heard the tractor and began trotting toward the opposite fence. Luke moved smoothly around them and opened the next gate. The cattle flowed through, lumbering to the long string of greenish feed mounded on the snow. A hint of sage blended with the smell of the hay. Luke rode back to where J.J. and Fawn plodded across the field and led them toward a gate that bordered the road.

J.J. preferred never speaking to him again, but something he'd started to say earlier nagged her. "What did you think?'' she asked. At his blank look, she elaborated. "You said when you saw me you thought, and then you stopped.''

Closing the gate behind them, Luke turned his horse in the direction of the ranch house. "About five years ago Zane was out riding, and his horse stepped in a prairie dog hole and somersaulted.'' Luke painstakingly adjusted each finger of his leather gloves. "Zane was laying flat on the ground when I found him. When the horse went over, the saddle horn crushed Zane's rib cage. Did all kinds of internal damage.''

His mechanical tone of voice prepared J.J. for what was coming.

"He died right after I found him.''

"I'm so sorry.'' The words sounded sadly inadequate.

Watching his uncle die and unable to do anything to help him must have been agonizing for Luke. The dry recitation of facts failed to hide Luke's grief. He rode to her left and J.J. reached awkwardly over and gently touched his hand where it rested on his right thigh. He stiffened, and she jerked back her hand, gluing it with her other hand to the saddle horn.

"All Zane said to me was, 'It wasn't Charlie's fault.' Then he died. I think he made himself hang on until somebody found him so he could say those words."

"Charlie?"

"Zane's favorite horse, named after the painter, Charles M. Russell. Zane was a fan of Russell's work." After a minute Luke added, "Mom couldn't bear to look at Charlie after that. She wanted me to shoot him. We had a big argument when I turned him out to pasture. Last summer, when he was twenty-two, I found him dead in a patch of wildflowers. Buried him so the scavengers couldn't get him." Luke didn't look at J.J. "I figure he and Zane are together again, trailing cows somewhere."

Moved by the sentiment behind Luke's last words, J.J. clung to the saddle horn and stared straight ahead, moisture blurring her vision. A hand pressed down on hers and then lifted so quickly she might have imagined it. Turning away from Luke, J.J. surreptitiously wiped away a tear rolling down her cheek.

The rumble of the tractor faded away behind them. A small earth-toned bird flew from the barbed-wire fence into a low bush. The sun moved west where clouds, building up over the Park Range, conspired to dim its brightness.

Durango nickered into the stark silence. Three crows standing in the middle of the road flapped into the air, cawing raucously. Durango snorted and shied, his ears flicking toward the large black birds. Luke sat loose-limbed in the saddle as the reddish gelding, his tail flying

high, drummed a fretful tattoo on the snowy roadbed.
To J.J.'s extreme relief, Fawn obeyed her frantic sawing
on the reins and stopped well out of range of Durango's
skittish hooves. Durango humped his spine one last time,
then looked back at Luke and shook his long head as if
bragging of chasing off the crows.

Luke laughed. "You crazy cayuse. Had to shake the
fidgets out of your legs, did you?"

His laughter eased the painful shadows from his eyes.
His broad smile played havoc with J.J.'s insides. "You
were both just showing off," she said tartly, telling herself any unsettled feelings in her stomach were caused
by envy of his riding skills. And sympathy for the way
he'd discovered his dying uncle. Her lying on the ground
must have instantly recalled the scene to Luke. "I'm
sorry for frightening you. I kind of shouted at the cows
and startled Fawn. She jumped and I..." J.J. shrugged.

"Smoothly dismounted," Luke suggested in a dead-
pan voice.

"The dismount might have been smooth, but the landing sure wasn't. My entire backside is going to be black
and blue tomorrow." Her twanging thigh muscles told
her bruises weren't going to be her only problem.

"What you need," Luke said, "is a good hot soak."

The large, gray horse looked at them and shook his head.

"No way." J.J. backed away from Luke. "I'm not
going anywhere that requires me to get on a horse."
When he'd handed her a T-shirt and a pair of his sweats
and told her to put them on along with warm outdoor
clothing because he had a surprise for her, nothing had
been said about horses. "I plan to spend half the night
soaking in a hot tub. I only had time for a quick shower
before I fixed dinner tonight."

She turned toward the house, taking one quick step
before Luke snagged the back collar of the sheepskin
coat she wore. Planting her feet firmly, in disbelief J.J.

watched her boots plow twin furrows in the snow as Luke dragged her backward away from the house, her legs trailing uselessly out in front of her. "Luke Remington, you let go of me this instant or you'll be sorry."

"Whacha gonna do, lawyer lady? Attack me with elk antlers?"

"I should have let Birdie's husband chop you into hamburger." Reaching down, she grabbed handfuls of snow and hurled them over her shoulders. When that produced nothing but derisive laughter, J.J. twisted around and grabbed Luke's legs.

Losing his balance, Luke toppled to the ground, releasing J.J.'s jacket. She dropped like a stone. Recovering quickly, she rolled over and struggled to her hands and knees. Luke was quicker. Before she could stand, he'd picked her up bodily from the ground and heaved her over his shoulder. She drew back to kick him, and felt a solid bulk behind her leg. A solid bulk that snorted and quivered. J.J. went very still.

"Wise move, O'Brien. You don't want to irritate Soldier."

"I don't want to anything Soldier," she hissed.

Luke stood her on her feet, penning her between his body and the horse. "You going to ride sitting up, or slung over him like a saddle blanket?" The amusement in his eyes glinted clearly in the glow from the ranch floodlights.

"I'm not riding—okay, sitting up!" she half shrieked as Luke hefted her up in the air. Throwing J.J.'s right leg across the horse, he plunked her on its back. J.J. grabbed for the saddle horn and made a terrifying discovery. "Luke, there's no saddle on this horse. What am I supposed to hold on to?" The next second she dove for the horse's neck, clutching frantically as Luke lightly vaulted up behind her.

Holding the reins in one hand, Luke urged Soldier slowly forward. "Take it easy, O'Brien." He loosened her death grip on the horse and pulled her against him, wrapping an arm around her waist. "Relax. I'm not going to let you fall. Soldier's part Tennessee walker. Riding him's like sitting in a rocking chair."

Maybe the horse didn't hammer pain through her body with his every step, but she wasn't about to admit it. "You can brutally force me to get on this horse, Luke Remington, but you can't make me like it."

Luke brought Soldier to a dead stop. After a second, Luke turned the horse in the direction they'd come from. In front of the house, he halted Soldier. "Go on back to the house if you're too chicken to come."

"What?" J.J. swiveled her head around to look at Luke. "You mean you'll let me get off this mangy beast and go in the house and you won't move a muscle to stop me?"

"Yes."

"Why?" she asked suspiciously.

"If you don't want to go with me, I'm not going to force you. I don't want you coming with me because I'm bigger and stronger than you. I don't want you coming because you're too afraid of me not to come."

"I'm not afraid of you," J.J. retorted. The horse shifted his rear end and stamped a hind foot. Caught by surprise, J.J. slid to one side. Luke's arms immediately tightened protectively about her waist, an action that yanked from J.J.'s subconscious an astonishing revelation. From the moment Luke Remington had thrust her from the path of a runaway horse, on some level she'd instinctively trusted him.

Which went a long way toward explaining her hasty marriage. With Luke she'd felt secure enough to act impulsively, to be someone other than the all-business, practical, clearheaded, cool-thinking, ambitious lawyer she was. For one week, the safety and security she'd known in his embrace had permitted her to explore a world without man-made boundaries. For which she'd always be grateful.

And she knew as well as she knew her own name, that she could have put a stop to his caveman behavior anytime she'd wanted to, but she wasn't about to let some no-account cowpoke claim lady lawyers lacked intestinal fortitude. Besides, curiosity had always been her besetting sin. J.J. raised her chin and crossed her arms in front of her. "I'm not chicken and I'd never be afraid of an arrogant, muscle-bound cowboy. If you've got something to show me, show me, so I can get back to a hot bath."

Wordlessly Luke nudged Soldier into motion.

Used to traffic noises and frenetic city lights, at first J.J. found the total silence and absolute darkness strange and eerie. Slowly her senses adjusted to the night. Snow frosted the distant dark mountains with an otherworldly pale blue. Overhead, stars sparkled as if they were diamonds on navy blue velvet. Leaning her head back against Luke's shoulder, she picked out the Big Dipper and the North Star. A half-moon bathed the landscape with pale light, casting weed-shaped shadows on the snow.

From a nearby field came the sound of cows lowing. Soldier snuffled, and the rhythmic clopping of his hooves mingled with the jangling of his bridle. Rustling noises along the road disclosed the presence of small creatures.

J.J. smelled the horse and the sage and the cold. And occasionally, when Luke moved, a whiff of the scent she associated with him. Eau de male. Giving in to temptation, J.J. relaxed against his chest and puzzled over why he'd turned back toward the ranch house.

The answer, when it came to her, stunned her. "You don't seriously think there's the slightest bit of similarity between you and Ad Parker, do you?"

"I wouldn't like to think so," Luke said in a level voice.

"Ad Parker likes people to be afraid of him, to cringe when they see him. Scaring people gives him a high similar to what other people get from drugs. Deep inside he's a coward. He doesn't know how to be a man, so he has to knock other people, smaller people, weaker people, down to prop himself up." When Luke didn't respond, J.J. added, "He'd never turn a horse out to pasture to enjoy his last days." She paused. "And he wouldn't comfort a woman who'd had a nightmare."

Luke guided the horse toward a pasture gate. "Hang on while I get this." He swung down and crunched through the snow, unfastening the gate and pushing it through a drift until he had an opening wide enough to lead Soldier through.

J.J. clung to the horse's mane, and said loudly. "You are a pain in the neck, obnoxious, overbearing, arrogant, overly fond of having your own way and think you're always right. You irritate me, infuriate me, make me mad, make me want to slug you and drive me absolutely crazy. You do not scare me. I don't care how much you yell at me or flex your muscles, I am not afraid of you, Luke Remington. You know why?"

Luke closed the gate and swung back on the horse. "Why?"

"Because I know I could trust you with my life. I would even let you take my nephews on the merry-go-round. Is that clear?"

"Very clear." He put his arms around her and told his horse to move. "You know that stuff you said about me irritating you, making you mad and so on? Ditto."

"Good. We understand each other." She settled back against his solid chest, feeling rather than hearing Luke's snort of laughter. Soldier picked his way by moonlight across the snowy pasture. J.J. sniffed. "Yuck. What is that awful smell? It smells like rotten eggs."

"Sulfur," Luke said, as if that explained everything.

J.J. sat up straight on the horse. "Luke, look. There's a fire up there. How can anything burn in all this snow? Look at the smoke pouring out of there."

Luke drew Soldier to a halt and slid off his back. He tied the horse's reins to a nearby bush. "It's not a fire." Clasping J.J. around her waist, he set her on the ground, turning her to face the gray clouds rising from the ground. "Your bath awaits."

"My bath?" Comprehension dawned. "A hot spring?"

"It comes out of a fissure in the rock alongside the creek." He held out his hand. "Come on."

They walked into the warm steam and entered another world. Clouds of moisture swirled around J.J.'s head. Beneath her feet the snow-free ground looked green and lush. Ahead of her flat rocks rimmed a pool about ten feet across. Other flat rocks terraced one side of the pool, as if they were stadium bleachers.

Luke took a folded plastic bag from his pocket. "Put in here whatever clothes you take off." He raised a mocking eyebrow. "I figured I couldn't talk you into skinny-dipping."

"Why not? You've managed to talk me into everything else you wanted me to do." She could have kicked herself for speaking without thinking. Luke would think she wanted him to persuade her to strip naked. She knew if he could see the color of her face, it would be bright red.

"Maybe I was a mite hasty loaning you my T-shirt."

"Too bad." Slipping out of her boots, she unzipped her jacket. "You're not getting it back." Shoving her outer garments into the plastic bag, J.J. turned her back to Luke and stripped down to his T-shirt over her underwear. A faint splash behind her told her Luke had beat her into the pool. She started to turn, then froze. Luke hadn't said whether or not he planned to skinny-dip. She didn't care if the pool covered the entire state of Colorado, she couldn't get in it if Luke soaked stark naked. The thought sent shivers though her body in spite of the warm steam surrounding her.

"Come on in, the water's fine," Luke said. "The temperature's about one hundred degrees."

"I'll be there in a minute." Crouching down, her back to Luke, she fussed with her clothing inside the plastic bag, precisely refolding each item over and over again.

"Chicken," Luke taunted softly.

"I'm not chicken. Why would I be? I can swim."

"Even if you couldn't, you'd be hard-pressed to drown. It's less than four feet at the deepest part, and you can sit on these rocks and go in only as deep as you want."

J.J. carefully smoothed the plastic bag over her clothes. "What are you wearing?"

CHAPTER NINE

"If you had any hair on your chest, O'Brien, you wouldn't ask," Luke drawled. "You'd turn around and see for yourself."

"Assuming you're equating hair on your chest with courage," J.J. retorted, spinning around, "I have plenty." Luke was little more than a misty shape in the steam. J.J. stomped over to the water and got her first clear view of him. Coming to an abrupt halt, she sucked in half the steam around the pool. Sulfurous steam that immediately sent her into a paroxysm of coughing.

Luke rose to his feet, moonlit water streaming down the well-shaped body J.J. remembered all too well. "Are you okay?"

"I'm fine. Get back in the pool before you catch your death of cold." Her toes curled in the grass. As if any germ would dare attack a healthy male specimen such as Luke. How many times did she have to see his bare chest before she quit reacting to it as if it were a pubescent female? Swallowing the last of her coughs, J.J. concentrated far more than necessary on not tripping on the rock steps down into the water.

"If the sulfur smell makes you sick, we don't—"

"I said I was fine. Something went down the wrong way." She wasn't about to admit the first thought to cross her mind at the sight of Luke lolling against the side of the pool, his damp shoulders glistening and water droplets clinging to his chest hairs, had been she hoped he wasn't wearing a stitch. Her second thought had been the one she'd choked on. Sulfur fumes must induce erotic fantasies.

Above the waterline, her bare feet encountered damp, furry-coated rocks. She stepped down, the warm water lapping sensuously at her legs, luring her deeper into the pool. A small wave broke across the surface as Luke sat.

He'd gone deeper, the water level almost to his chin as he stretched out, a rock behind him pillowing his head. Watching her descend into the water, he said, "After a few minutes you'll get used to the smell and won't even notice it."

She'd already forgotten the smell. What she was trying not to notice was the large, scantily clad male who shared the pool. J.J. wiggled around on the rocks, seeking a comfortable place to sit. Following Luke's example, she leaned her head back against a slanted rock. The warm water soothed her muscles. The heated desire racing through her veins proved not the least bit soothing. Her mind wanted to run screaming back to the ranch. Her body wanted to float over and merge with Luke's.

Her toes drifted up to the water's surface, and she studied them with great intensity as she searched for a safe topic of conversation. The skimpy amount of blue fabric hugging Luke's lean hips when he'd stood didn't seem all that safe to discuss. Closing her eyes failed to erase the image from her mind.

"You getting things settled for Birdie?"

It took J.J. a minute to realize Luke had asked her something. She moved her thoughts away from forbidden channels. "Based on Birdie's affidavit claiming domestic violence, the court issued a temporary restraining order and a citation for a domestic violence hearing. No matter what happens there, I'm going to file a petition with the district court for dissolution of Birdie's marriage. She'll be seeking custody of Jackie Ann."

"Ad's not going to like that."

"Ad Parker's likes and dislikes concern me not one whit."

"Birdie go home to her folks?"

"No. She had a friend pick her and the baby up at the hospital and take them to a safe place. I offered, but she was afraid Ad might be watching me. She planned to call someone she thought her husband would never think of." J.J. drew circles in the water. "I can't imagine not being able to call on your own family for help."

"Me, neither. My dad and I don't always see eye to eye, but I know he wants the best for me, even if we never agree what that is. I've never doubted he'll stand by me, no matter what."

"He still in the army?"

"Remingtons don't leave the army unless they die or are forced out because of age," Luke said dryly. "My dad, his dad, all the way back to before the Civil War. I was slated to be the sixth General Remington."

"I guess that explains why you're so bossy. General Remington, sir!" Water cascaded from J.J.'s mock salute.

"I'm not bossy. You're just allergic to listening to any suggestions a man has."

"I know all about males and their 'suggestions.' I have four brothers. If I hadn't kicked and scratched and fought every breathing moment of every single day, they would have used me for their own personal doormat. Cinderella would have had nothing on me. My mom told me early on fairy godmothers were out of fashion. She said whatever I decided to do with my life was fine with her, except I had to be able to take care of myself, whatever happens."

Luke shifted, in the process splashing J.J.'s face. He reached over, wiping away the droplets and drew her damp hair behind her ear. "Does your mom think you can take care of yourself?"

"She worries she did too good a job convincing me. She thinks I'm too independent." Her mom should have told her how to take care of herself when the sexiest cowboy in creation sat inches away, his finger lightly tracing the whorls of her ear.

"She's right."

"You say that because you're a man. Men are afraid of independent women." Meant to ridicule, her words came out more like a sultry challenge.

Luke chuckled. "I'll bet you're a good lawyer." His next words erased any notion J.J. might have had that he'd complimented her. "The mind always working, the mouth always going."

A lot of J.J.'s parts were working and going right now. None of them happened to be her mind or her mouth. The front of the T-shirt she wore had trapped a minuscule amount of air that caused the fabric to float above her body. Luke's every little movement sent tiny waves across the surface of the pond. Waves that lapped against J.J. and caused the T-shirt to barely brush her sensitized skin. To think some misguided people thought hot mineral pools were relaxing.

Obviously Luke was one of them. "Those stiff muscles loosening up, O'Brien?"

"Sure," she lied in a tight voice.

"Doesn't look like it to me." He slid closer. "Let me work on those legs." Before J.J. could grasp his intention, he hoisted her legs onto his lap and began rubbing her upper thighs. "Relax. You're as stiff as a board."

Relax! The man was deranged. How could she possibly relax when his touch set her afire. The heat raging through her veins had nothing to do with the temperature of the water. "Luke, I don't think this is a good idea."

"No? Then tell me to stop, lawyer lady." Suddenly the way he kneaded her flesh had little to do with sore muscles.

"I can't," she whispered.

"That's good, O'Brien," he drawled with deep satisfaction. Sliding his hands under the T-shirt, he lifted her onto his lap. "I'm not sure I could stop."

J.J.'s few pieces of clothing floated away to slowly sink to the bottom of the pool.

Much later, J.J. idly drew her foot through the water. "I should have known you'd figure out someway to get me to skinny-dip." The silken water caressed her torpid body.

"I wanted to take your mind off your sore muscles," Luke said virtuously, running his hand over her bare hip.

"Mmm, I think you succeeded. At least for the moment. Luke—" she wove her fingers through his chest hair, pausing to curl a crisp hair around her index finger "—I've been here over a week. Why did you wait so long to show me the hot spring?"

"Why do you think?"

"I think you didn't tell me before because you knew we'd end up doing what we did. So why tonight?"

"You have to ask me that after the way you attacked me in the pasture this afternoon?"

"I wondered if that was it." Cupping her hand, she scooped up water and poured it slowly over Luke's shoulder.

His hand tightened on her hip. "Regrets?"

J.J. ladled more water over him. "No." The water ran in little rivulets down Luke's chest. "Maybe." She dipped her hand back into the water. "I don't know." She targeted one of Luke's nipples with water droplets. "I don't know what gets into me when I'm around you. Things like skinny-dipping are totally foreign to my nature." J.J. slid away from him and moved across the pool, collecting their clothing, then waded back to the terraced rocks where Luke reclined. Handing him his briefs, she squeezed the water from her clothing. "I've never been the type who strips naked outdoors to do anything."

Luke grinned at her wryly perplexed voice. "I don't suppose it's the sort of behavior lawyer ladies indulge in."

Lack of clothing wasn't the real issue, but J.J. couldn't bring herself to discuss the physical attraction that once again brought about their downfall. She climbed up the rocks. "These wet clothes are going to be miserable to wear home."

"You won't need them under the sweat suit. Put the wet stuff in the bag." He handed her a towel, and J.J. quickly dried off and dressed. Before she could put on her knit cap, Luke pulled her toward him and roughly toweled her short, damp hair. "I should have noticed you were getting it wet. Be sure you cover every single wet hair with your hat." He led the way through the clouds of steam to where he'd tied the horse.

J.J. sat behind Luke, clinging to his waist, as they rode silently back to the ranch house through the star-filled night. Once, he halted Soldier and pointed. Two mule deer, their large ears alertly erect, stood stock-still, staring at horse and humans. When Luke nudged Soldier to move on, the deer abruptly turned and bounded away, their upraised tails flagging white in the pale moonlight. Proving they had more sense than J.J. They ran from danger; they didn't move in with it.

Clouds hung low with the promise of snow as J.J. descended the courthouse steps. Filing Birdie's various motions with the court had taken longer than she'd anticipated. Luke would be at the diner waiting. No doubt eating the last piece of banana pie. It seemed Susan always saved one slice of banana pie for Luke. Outsiders had to make do with whatever regulars didn't want.

And J.J. definitely belonged in the outsider category. She could hardly wait to escape back to Denver where she belonged. Where she was wanted. No one wanted her here.

Luke's behavior since their lovemaking in the thermal pool two nights ago clearly illustrated he regretted their actions. Not only had he not so much as stolen a teasing kiss since, but he no longer insisted J.J. spend every waking moment with him. No waking moment, in fact. No more requests to help feed the cattle. No more horse-back rides. He showed up for meals and shut himself in his office after dinner. Were it anyone but Luke, she'd suspect him of inventing excuses to stay away from her.

He'd barricaded himself behind an impersonal civility J.J. found impossible to pierce. The past two nights she'd considered walking into his bedroom and tossing his rea-soning back at him, that overexposure would kill off their physical attraction for each other. The realization Luke no longer felt attracted to her held her back. What if he kicked her out, or worse yet, what if he let her stay out of pity?

J.J. pulled her down coat snugly around her and set off toward the diner. She wasn't keen about facing Susan again, but Luke's suggestion they meet at the diner when they'd finished their individual business had been deliv-ered in a challenging manner. J.J. had never excelled at backing away from a challenge.

Her steps lagged. She'd never been one to back away from facing the truth, either. Yet that's exactly what she'd been doing the past few days.

She didn't want it to happen; she didn't know how it happened. It made absolutely no sense whatsoever. None of which changed the basic truth. She loved a man who was totally wrong for her. They had nothing in common. Their goals in life were at the ends of divergent paths. They couldn't be more ill suited for each other.

Chaotic thoughts bounced around in her head as she slowly walked toward the diner, brooding over Luke's good qualities. The respect he commanded in the area. The way he'd helped Tony and Sal. The way he took crises in stride, from runaway horses to early babies. The way he'd deliberately put himself in danger to protect Birdie from her husband. The affectionate way he talked about his uncle. His slow, sexy way of moving that seemed so effortless, yet accomplished so much. The way his hazel eyes changed when he was amused. When he made love.

J.J. mentally slapped herself, deliberately recalling each and every instance of Luke's stubborn, pigheadedness. Luke didn't want her kind of wife. He wanted a wife on his terms. Terms J.J. couldn't live with. She'd worked too hard, gained too much, to give up everything for hazel eyes and a sexy smile. Especially when the owner of those eyes and smile showed absolutely no inclination to give up anything for her.

Burton wouldn't expect to come before everything else in her life. He wouldn't want J.J. to conform, to compromise, to yield, to subordinate her life to his. He admired her independence.

She thought about Burton's statement that he couldn't love her if she loved Luke and promptly dismissed it. Burton still loved his Caroline. He didn't need to know about J.J.'s temporary aberration. How long could it take to fall out of love with a man who didn't love you?

"Well, well, well, if it isn't Mrs. Luke Remington, the big city lawyer who sticks her snooty nose where it don't belong."

Lost in her thoughts, J.J. had paid no attention to passersby. She realized her error too late. Ad Parker stood on the sidewalk before her, blocking her path. His breath reeked of alcohol. Hoping to avoid a public confrontation, J.J. nodded her head civilly, said, "Hello, Mr. Parker," and started around him.

He stepped sideways, countering her attempt to pass. "Where's my wife and kid?"

"It's not my place to give you that information."

"You know. Where'd you hide 'em?" He stepped closer in a blatant attempt to intimidate her.

J.J. stood her ground. "My advice to you, Mr. Parker, would be for you to consult your lawyer."

"You can take your advice and shove it. I want Bird and my kid."

His dirty, uncombed hair, unshaven face and disgusting breath made J.J. want to gag. "Excuse me, Mr. Parker, I'm late for an appointment." She moved to one side.

He grabbed her arm, squeezing it hard. "I asked you a question. Where's my wife?"

He wouldn't assault her in broad daylight in the middle of town. "I suggest you take your hand off me, Mr. Parker," she said as calmly as she could. "You aren't doing yourself or your situation any good by behaving in this manner."

His whole face curled up in a sneer. "Maybe knocking you flat would do me good." He thrust his face into hers. "See how you like everyone in town laughing at you." He twisted her arm. "You shouldn't have gone around town bragging you took me down with those damned elk antlers."

J.J.'s knees wanted to knock together, but she stiffened them with sheer willpower. People like Ad Parker fed on fear. "If people are laughing, you ought to look at your own behavior."

"Shut up and listen to me and listen good," Parker snarled. "Being Mrs. Luke Remington ain't gonna save you. I'll find Bird and teach her a lesson about leaving her husband. Then I'm coming after you." He jerked J.J.'s arm hard. "An uppity city woman like you needs to learn her place."

"Threatening me won't do you any good."

"Parker!" Ev Bailey's voice came from across the street. "You're in enough trouble. Back off from Mrs. Remington."

Ad Parker had drunk enough alcohol to dull his brain and befuddle his wits. His eyeballs rolling wildly, he looked at the sheriff. "You back off, Sheriff. Me and Mrs. Remington are just having a friendly little talk."

He gave J.J.'s arm another painful yank. "Ain't that right, Mrs. Remington?"

"I think we're through talking," J.J. said evenly, her heart racing. She disliked the cunning smile on Parker's face. People gathered in the street, watching the little drama. J.J. wished they'd leave. Intuition told her Parker wouldn't back down in front of an audience. Perceiving himself as humiliated once by J.J., he wouldn't allow it to happen again.

A movement at her side, a quick glimpse of metal and J.J. felt the bottom drop out of her stomach. Parker had a gun. Ev walked toward them. Thinking fast, J.J. said, "You're not the type who needs to use a gun to make your point, Mr. Parker." She spoke quietly so as not to incite Parker into precipitate action. Ev's sudden halt told her the sheriff heard and understood her warning. Feeling Parker shift his body, J.J. knew he was raising the hand holding the gun. Her heart pounded.

"Sissies like Parker always use guns, O'Brien."

"I'll show you who's a sissy, Remington!" Parker forcibly shoved J.J. to the ground.

J.J. tried to scream at Luke to run, at Parker not to hurt Luke. Luke, who'd deliberately attracted Parker's angry, drunken focus to himself and away from J.J. Her paralyzed throat muscles refused to utter a sound. She could do nothing but sprawl on the sidewalk and watch in terror.

Nothing else was required. In the blink of an eye, Parker's gun clattered to the ground and he was rolling in the street, howling and holding his wrist.

Pulling out handcuffs, Ev ran across the street. A police car pulled up with two policemen. One jumped out, and he and Ev hustled a cuffed Parker into the back of the police car.

Luke helped a shaken J.J. to her feet. "You okay?" he asked, breathing hard.

She nodded, wanting nothing so much as to seek sanctuary in Luke's strong arms. Hysteria hovered close to the surface, but J.J. thrust it aside as the policeman turned to her. In a seemingly unending ordeal, she answered questions while he wrote down her answers. Occasionally others spoke. Finally the police car drove away with its prisoner.

"You were right. He had the safety on." Ev grinned at Luke. "And I was right. You're as quick as you were."

"Quick, hell. I felt as if I were wading through snowdrifts." Luke glowered at J.J. "Why are you rubbing your wrist?"

"I fell on it, but it's okay."

Luke bundled her down the street and into his pickup. "They can look at it at the clinic."

"I don't need to go to the clinic. I'm fine."

Luke pulled into the clinic parking lot. "They'll check it out."

"Did you hear me? I'm fine."

"Don't. Argue. I'm barely controlling my temper as it is."

Luke's rigid jaw and curt voice told her he wasn't kidding. "Why are you mad at me?"

"Because you're the one stupid enough to engage Parker in conversation. Didn't the fact he held a knife on Birdie and me the other night tell you anything at all about how unpredictable and vicious and dangerous he is? If he hadn't been so drunk he forgot he had the safety on, who knows how many people he could have shot." Luke gripped the steering wheel so tightly, his knuckles showed white. "Don't you dare tell me you could have handled him on your own."

"I wouldn't waste my breath." J.J. whipped up anger to melt the terror still sitting in her stomach like a block of ice. She jumped out of the pickup before Luke could walk around to open the passenger door. "I'm well aware you think me stupid enough to invite a deranged drunk to join us for tea.'' Sticking her chin in the air, she marched into the clinic.

Later, her wrist bandaged due to a slight sprain caused by her fall, J.J. stomped past Luke on her way back to the truck. She saw no point in wasting breath giving explanations to an opinionated cowboy who thought he knew everything.

A long arm snaked around her to hold shut the door J.J. was trying to open. ''Do you still want a piece of pie?''

''No.'' Her answer came out colder than the frozen snow on the ground.

''I think I better eat a piece of pie,'' Luke said ruefully. ''Humble pie. A big piece.'' Pulling J.J. backward against his chest, he held her close, one arm around her shoulders, the other encircling her below her breasts. ''Ev and I were in the diner when Jack came running in and said Parker had been drinking and making threats against you and then he saw you coming down the street. Jack said he thought Parker had a gun...'' His voice shook. ''I don't ever want to be that scared again.''

J.J. swung around, burying her face in Luke's sheepskin coat. ''You think you were scared... I was petrified, but then I heard your voice and I thought Luke's here and everything's okay, but then I got scared again because I knew you were giving him you as a target instead of Ev or me...'' Shuddering with the horror of what might have been, J.J. clung to Luke. He held her so tightly, she felt the large button on his coat marking her cheek.

After a few minutes of soaking up Luke's strength and comfort, J.J. lifted her head. ''I haven't even thanked you. You moved so fast...'' Ev's words came back to her. ''What did Ev mean about you being as quick as you were?''

''Special Forces.'' Luke opened the door and helped her up into the pickup.

"You were in the Special Forces? When?" J.J. asked as he swung in behind the wheel.

"Centuries ago, the way I aged today." When the look J.J. gave him told him she wanted more of an answer, he said, "I enlisted in the army after high school and ended up in Special Forces. If it hadn't been for the ranch, I might have made a career of it. Instead I stayed in long enough to prove to my dad I could hack it, then, instead of reupping, I came back to the ranch. Zane suggested I go to college to learn all the new ranching theories and range management techniques, so I put myself through with help from the G.I. bill." He gave her a quick glance. "How's your wrist?"

J.J. thought about Ad Parker flat on his back, moaning in the middle of the street, and she grinned at Luke. "Much better than Parker's wrist."

"I should have broken some of his bones," Luke said savagely, "lots of bones."

J.J. covertly studied Luke's hard-edged profile. The lethal look on his face demonstrated how thin man's veneer of civilization was, but she wasn't nearly as shocked as she should be. Sinking against the back of the seat, J.J. realized what truly shocked her was the immense satisfaction she felt at Luke's primitive reaction to a man threatening his wife. Even if she wasn't much of a wife.

Tall candles, short candles, fat candles, thin candles, square candles and round candles, candles of every color, not to mention two pumpkin-shaped candles and a candle that might be an owl, stood in cups, saucers and candle holders. J.J. doubted she'd missed a candle in her thorough search of the house. The massed candles blazed from every flat surface in the living room. A fire roared in the huge stone fireplace.

Outdoors, snow fell as darkness descended. Upstairs the sound of the shower had stopped some time ago.

Footsteps descended the stairs, and Luke stood at the outer edge of the candlelight. "What's with all the candles?"

J.J. lit the two stubby candles on the small card table set up on the cowhide rug in front of the fireplace. "I felt festive."

"Are we celebrating something?" Luke moved closer to survey the linen-covered table set with the best china J.J. could find.

"Sort of. That the situation in town this morning didn't end in a terrible tragedy."

"Worse things happen on Denver streets every day."

"Not to me," J.J. said. "I doubt Parker intended things to go as far as they did, but once he had an audience... I think he would have shot me and Ev, and who knows how many other people. You stopped that from happening. Thank you."

Luke gave her a dark, narrow-eyed look. "Let me guess. When you rushed in to supposedly rescue me from Parker, I didn't display the proper gratitude. This is your way of demonstrating how much more class you have, isn't it? Because we both know J. J. O'Brien doesn't appreciate men coming to her aid."

After taking a deep, calming breath, J.J. said carefully, "I realize I'm too independent for your tastes, and while it's true I prefer standing on my own two feet instead of relying on a man, I like to think I'm at least honest with myself. The truth is, I was absolutely terrified this morning."

"I'm sure you would have figured out a way to take out Parker, spare the town and save the world's population of whales."

J.J. grabbed the back of the nearest chair to keep from throwing something at Luke Remington. "I'm giving you a choice." She viciously squeezed the chair's leather padding. "You can graciously accept my thanks, or you can watch me dump the pot roast in the garbage."

A crooked smile greeted her words. "I wouldn't want to waste the pot roast. Not when it smells this good." He walked around the table and pulled out J.J.'s chair. "You don't owe me any thanks. Ev called the town police from the diner, but we knew it would take them a few minutes to get there. We hoped when Parker saw Ev he'd regain his senses. If he didn't." Luke shrugged, and sat across from J.J.

"Super Sarge to the rescue," J.J. finished. "That is why your uncle called you 'Sarge'? Because you were in the army? Were you a sergeant?"

"Yes." Luke devoted himself to filling his plate. "Dinner looks and smells delicious."

"I know the occasion calls for chateaubriand, but pot roast is the fanciest I cook."

"I like pot roast." Luke forked a hunk of meat. "I don't need anything fancy. You're making too big a deal out of what happened," he said to his plate.

"Saving my life may not be a big deal to you," J.J. retorted, "but it's a big deal to me. I'm sure Margo thinks it's a big deal you saved Ev's life."

"Ev can take care of himself. Damn it, O'Brien, eat."

J.J. started to argue, noticed the dusky stain on Luke's cheeks and the realization hit her. Luke wasn't being ungracious. The role of hero embarrassed him. Remembering his temper tantrum after she'd disarmed Parker in the kitchen, she couldn't resist teasing him. Tenting her hands over her plate, J.J. rested her chin on her fingertips and widened her eyes. "It was as if a Texas ranger had ridden in and saved the town. You can put another notch in your six-gun, cowboy."

Luke laid down his silverware and gave J.J. a dark look. "You know damned well I'm no hero. Ev and I regularly practice against each other so we don't completely lose our skills. I'm faster than him because he's got a bum leg. Now can we drop the subject before you ruin my dinner?"

J.J. changed the subject to Luke's days growing up in the military. He soon had her laughing at tales of life on army bases from Hawaii to the East Coast to Europe. "Not that I remember Hawaii," he admitted. "We moved from there before I was two. Those are stories my mom tells on me. How about you? I'll bet you moved a lot as your family grew."

"Wrong. My dad bought his grandparents' house in Des Moines, Iowa. A huge, rambling, run-down Second Empire Victorian. Dad had grand plans for fixing it up in his spare time." J.J. made a face. "As if a doctor with five kids has spare time. Family vacations consisted of short visits to relatives. My dad's parents lived a few blocks away, and Grandma and Grandpa Daniels lived in Ames. We had cousins all over the state of Iowa."

"Sounds like fun."

J.J. smiled. "The grass is always greener. I longed to travel. The highlight of my youth was a trip to Kansas City. The only things well traveled about me are my ancestors. I was born and raised in Iowa, traveled some in Kansas and Nebraska and now live in Colorado. I've never seen an ocean."

"You'll have to get Alexander to take you to Europe. Maybe you can go for your honeymoon. Or to Hawaii. When will our divorce be final?"

J.J. cut the remaining pot roast on her plate into tiny, precise pieces. "Once we file a petition with the courts for dissolution of our marriage, a date may be set for the final hearing. Since I'm an attorney, things are a little more complicated than usual, even though we have no children and neither of us are contesting the divorce. The court will probably want you to have an attorney representing your interests. The minimum cooling-off period is ninety days, but we'll be very lucky if we can get the final hearing set in under 120 days."

"You could be dancing the hula in Waikiki by late

summer. Or have you already decided where you're going on a honeymoon?"

"No."

"Mom told me I was conceived on an isolated beach on the island of Kauai. Maybe I ought to ask her where so you can start the next generation of Alexanders there."

J.J. drew in a sharp breath. "Carrie is the next generation of Alexanders."

"I'm talking about your children."

Mashing her carrots, J.J. stirred them into her potatoes. When Burton's wife, Caroline, became ill, the doctor forbid her to get pregnant again. Burton thought his wife had enough to deal with, so he'd taken steps to ensure he'd father no more children. He'd suggested adoption to J.J., but she knew his heart wasn't in it. None of which was Luke's business. J.J. fell back on the one benefit she'd convinced herself offset a childless future. "I don't plan to have children. They drain one's time and energy. I want to concentrate on my career."

"I see," Luke said contemptuously. "Children would definitely be an encumbrance to an up and coming attorney." He paused. "You're right about one thing. We have absolutely nothing in common. I want a family. And I want a wife who wants one, too."

Clenching her fists in her lap so tightly her fingernails bit into her palms, J.J. said, "I've never made any pretense about what I want from life. I could never be a wife like your mother. When we met, if you thought otherwise and that's why you married me, I'm sorry."

"At least the sex was good," Luke said crudely.

J.J. precisely stacked her dirty dishes. "Yes." She stood. "I found an apple pie in the freezer. Would you like a piece?"

"No." Luke shoved back from the table. "I'm through."

Through with dinner. Through with their sham of a

marriage. Through with J.J. He didn't love her. He loved his picture of the ideal wife. So much for her plans to seduce Luke tonight.

"I'll phone Burton," she said. "Tomorrow's Saturday. He can drive up and take me home." She'd accomplished what Luke had hoped for. He could no longer stand the sight of her.

Using her spoon, J.J. extinguished the candles around the room. And wished it were as easy to extinguish the pain that shattered her heart into a million pieces.

"Gosh, J.J., I didn't even know you were married until Daddy told me," Carrie said as they drove away from Luke's ranch. "A secret marriage is too cool and *soooo* romantic."

J.J. could think of a lot of things to call her marriage, but romantic wasn't one of them. An opinion obviously shared by her soon-to-be ex-husband who had not returned to the house after feeding the cattle this morning. J.J. had rejected Burton's suggestion they wait for Luke before leaving.

The last thing she wanted was Burton's daughter viewing J.J.'s disastrous first marriage as the world's greatest love story. She turned to the young girl in the back seat. "Did you know a romance used to be defined as a story of a knight's heroic adventures?" When Carrie shook her head, J.J. said, "Once when I went to visit your mom after she'd lost her hair from chemotherapy, she was modeling wigs for you and your dad and making jokes and laughing. She was very brave for you and your dad because she loved you so much. That's my idea of romantic."

Carrie rapidly blinked her eyes. "You think my mom was a hero?" She added in a little voice, "Me, too."

Burton cleared his throat. "Carrie and I were up before the chickens this morning having breakfast. I thought we'd lunch in Winter Park, but maybe we can pick up some doughnuts here to stave off starvation.''

Knowing Burton's love of pie, J.J. suggested Susan Curtis's diner and prayed she wouldn't find Luke there.

Susan sat behind the empty counter reading a book. ''Morning.'' Setting a mug in front of J.J., Susan filled it with coffee, then looked over J.J.'s shoulder. ''Where's Luke?''

''Working,'' J.J. said. ''I brought some friends in for pie. Burton Alexander and his daughter, Carrie. Burton, Carrie, this is Susan Curtis. I can recommend Susan's apple pie.''

Burton read the menu of pies on the blackboard. ''Banana cream for me. I haven't had it in ages. And decaf coffee.''

''Sorry. Only two pieces of banana cream left. J.J. gets one, and the other's spoken for.'' Susan put a slice of pie in front of J.J. ''Thanks for being in Birdie's corner. When it comes to a husband abusing his wife, too many people look the other way.''

Totally at a loss for words, caused as much by Susan's actions as by what she'd said, J.J. settled for a shrug.

''The insurance office down the street is going to be vacant next month. Ted's closing up, said he's taking his old bones to Arizona. I can tell him when he comes in to hold it until you look at it, J.J.'' Susan added, ''I'm sure it's not what you're used to, but you won't need a fancy law office around here.''

J.J. took such a large swallow of coffee she scalded her mouth. ''Water,'' she gasped. She drank the cooling liquid while Susan waited on Burton and Carrie.

''So, Burt—I assume you go by Burt?''

''No, I answer to Burton,'' he said pleasantly.

Susan raised an eyebrow. ''Ah, a city boy.''

''No, a city man.''

''Pretty sure of yourself, aren't you?'' Susan leaned her elbows on the counter. ''I suppose you're rich.''

He threw her a challenging look. "I could buy and sell you."

J.J. choked on another swallow of coffee, scarcely able to believe what was happening before her very eyes. Burton and Susan managed to load every word, every look, every gesture between them with sexual overtones. J.J. couldn't remember ever before seeing Burton come on to a woman other than Caroline.

Susan refilled J.J.'s water glass without taking her eyes off Burton. "Married?"

Burton carved a bite of apple pie with his fork. "My wife died of cancer two years ago."

Susan briefly touched the back of his hand. "I'm sorry." She turned to Carrie. "More milk?"

They were halfway to Winter Park before Burton mentioned Susan. "Nice lady. It would be interesting to know her story."

"A drunk driver killed her husband and two little boys five years back. Three years ago she moved to North Park."

"She seemed to think you were staying with Remington."

"She thought wrong."

CHAPTER TEN

BURTON stood at the window, watching the busy Friday night traffic outside J.J.'s town house. "I know I sent you up there, but I never expected this. I wish I could be sure you're not resigning because you're concerned about my feelings."

J.J. moved to his side and lightly squeezed his arm. "You're one of my dearest friends, which is why I won't marry you, but my decision to leave the firm has nothing to do with you."

"You've worked hard to get where you are. Why throw it away on a whim?"

"It's not a whim. I hardly know how to explain it, but when Ad Parker menaced me..." J.J. barely repressed a shudder. "It was broad daylight, in the middle of town, people around, yet I felt so helpless and vulnerable. For the first time, I understood what life must be like for people such as Birdie who are victimized by those bigger or stronger than they are."

"You can't save all the Birdies of the world."

"I may not even be able to save Birdie. I connected her with a domestic abuse center here in Denver, but she is going to have to make some hard choices about her future. Parker violated his restraining order and is facing charges from attacking me, but he could get off with a slap on the wrist. We both know the courts can't guarantee Parker will never hurt Birdie again."

"She could even return to her husband. Victims of domestic abuse frequently do."

"I know, but that doesn't change the fact that a lot of people need someone on their side with the skills to fight for them. Maybe I can't do much to help, but I have to try."

"You help people at our law firm."

"The kind of clients who come to your firm can always find help. The people I want to help need a lawyer who doesn't intimidate them or own a desk that cost more than their house."

"Where do you plan to practice?"

"Maybe in Denver. Maybe I'll check around for a small town looking for an attorney. I haven't decided yet."

Burton turned to study the painting hanging on the wall. "I'd understand it easier if you were staying married to Remington and moving into that office Susan mentioned."

"Don't make me think all the gender sensitivity training I've lavished on you has been wasted," J.J. teased. "Women can make decisions based on something besides a man."

"You said you love him." He gestured at the wall.

J.J. followed his gaze to the painting of Luke and Durango she'd splurged on. Unwisely. Hazel eyes already haunted her dreams. "Love takes two," she said flatly.

The package, delivered Saturday by a local service, came from the art gallery whose opening had brought Luke back into her life. A tear in the brown wrapping revealed the pioneer woman's blue bonnet. J.J. ripped away the rest of the paper.

Burton must have seen her admiring the watercolor and bought it for her as a belated birthday present. A dismaying second possibility occurred to J.J. Or for a wedding gift. He'd undoubtedly forgotten about the painting in the emotional uproar of J.J. refusing to marry him combined with her resigning from the law firm. Naturally she'd return it.

A small white envelope taped to the back of the painting caught J.J.'s eye. Removing the envelope, she propped the watercolor on her fireplace mantel and sat on the sofa, her gaze locked on the painting, her earlier pleasure in the watercolor rekindled. So much hope, strength and courage shone from the woman's face.

J.J. opened the envelope, extracted a white card and read the few words written on it. She blinked and read them again. "To O'Brien from Luke Remington." It wasn't Luke's handwriting. Someone at the gallery had written it.

J.J. studied the card as if she could ferret out its hidden meaning. Luke's sending the painting made no sense. A man didn't give an expensive gift to the woman he planned to divorce.

All at once the significance of the gift struck her. She looked at the watercolor again. Only this time through Luke's eyes. Luke wouldn't see the strength. He'd see what he wanted to see—a woman who'd followed her husband unquestioningly into the wilderness. He'd sent the painting as an insulting reminder of the kind of wife he wanted. The kind J.J. could never be. Anger, borne of hurt, boiled inside her.

J.J. crushed the card and hurled it across the room toward the fireplace. The crumpled paper bounced off the closed glass fireplace doors. Burning the card wouldn't erase the taunt. She couldn't bring herself to destroy the painting. She'd return it to Luke.

Personally.

The closer to Luke's ranch she came, the more heated grew the battle J.J. waged between anger and pain. She'd loved him, trusted him, and he'd repaid her with an ugly gesture akin to thumbing his nose at her deepest feelings. If she didn't like the watercolor too much to destroy it, she'd smash it over an arrogant, single-minded, pigheaded, self-righteous, condescending, chauvinistic head.

Driving too fast, she almost missed the turn to the ranch. Her car's tires spun on the snow-packed road, sending the car skidding toward the ditch. Warding off disaster at the last possible moment, J.J. slowed to enter the ranch yard.

Near the barn, an older woman hefted hay bales onto the sled. Ethel must have returned. The tractor engine clattered into operation. Sunlight reflecting off the tractor's windshield hid the driver—Jeff or Dale going out for the afternoon feeding. Stepping from the car, J.J. slammed the door. Luke must be in the barn. Before she could head in that direction, out of the corner of her eye she caught movement at his bedroom window.

Snatching the painting, J.J. charged into the house and up the stairs. She skidded to a halt as a tall, gorgeous brunette emerged from the bathroom. The woman's damp, wavy hair hung down to the top of the brown bath towel wrapped loosely around her body. "Who are you?" J.J. blurted out. She had expected Luke to find another woman. She hadn't expected him to find one so soon. She hadn't expected it to hurt so much.

The brunette arched a well-shaped brow. "Who are you?"

"I'm Luke's wife."

The woman's eyes widened in surprise. "You're not what I expected," she said in a low, husky voice edged with animosity.

J.J. preferred not to think about how Luke had described her to this woman. The watercolor pulled heavily on her arm, reminding her of the purpose of her visit. She pivoted on her heel, heading for Luke's bedroom. Ripping off the wrapping paper, J.J. leaned the painting against the middle of the bed's headboard.

The brunette surveyed the watercolor before casually pushing it to one side, making room for her to recline on the bed. The towel rode up, exposing the tops of long, lovely legs. "What's with the artwork?"

"I'm returning it," J.J. said curtly. She hated the woman. And knew the brunette had never in her life worn a business suit.

"Why? Is it Luke's?" The woman curled Luke's name around her tongue as if it were a decadent chocolate truffle.

"Ask Luke why. If I were you, I'd do it before I crawled between the sheets with him." As if the woman hadn't already crawled there.

"Honey, you're not me."

Someone ought to choke the fake Southern drawl out of the woman. J.J. bared her teeth in a malicious smile. "A fact Luke will regret each and every time he makes love to you."

The brunette gave J.J. a startled look, then started giggling. At J.J.'s outraged look, the giggles turned to laughter.

J.J. wheeled. Gales of hilarity followed her from the room, down the stairs and out the front door. Fighting back tears, J.J. ran for her car.

"O'Brien!" Luke's clarion yell came from the barn.

J.J. didn't break stride. Whipping around the tractor lumbering across the ranch yard, she raced toward her car. The stupid door wouldn't open. She pulled and yanked and beat on the handle until it dawned on her she'd automatically locked it when she got out, forgetting she wasn't in the city. Fumbling with her key, J.J. opened the door and scrambled in behind the steering wheel. A quick glance in the rearview mirror showed Luke running toward her. She couldn't face him. Not when he had a woman in his bedroom. The car balked at starting, but finally the engine caught. J.J. took another quick peek in the mirror. Luke was still too far away to reach her.

Remembering her earlier skid on the icy snow, she

gave the car as much gas as she dared and carefully made her way toward the gate. Half her mind on her driving, the other half trying to convince herself she didn't care if Luke slept with most of the beautiful women in Colorado, J.J. failed to see the tractor bearing down on her until the roar of the huge machine forcibly alerted her to its presence.

A man she'd never seen gestured from the tractor for her to pull over. Shaking her head, J.J. steered straight ahead. At the Stirling gate, the sharp turn onto the road forced her to reduce speed, and the tractor closed the distance between them. Slowly, almost gently, mimicking Durango moving a cow, the tractor driver hazed J.J.'s car into a bank of snow.

Stuck solid, the car refused to budge. J.J. turned it off, wrenched open the door and stormed back to the tractor as its engine died away. Ignoring the cold snow invading her shoes, she shouted up to the driver. "What are you, some kind of raving maniac? Get my car out of there right now, you stupid jerk."

The man looked down his nose at her. "Don't you scream at me like that, young lady. I'm General—"

"I don't care if you're the king of Siam," J.J. yelled, cutting him off. "Pull out my car!"

Luke trotted up as a strident whistle pierced the air. The brunette, still wearing the towel, hung out Luke's bedroom window. "Anyone who stands up to the general is a keeper," the woman yelled. "Don't let her get away."

"Sara Anne Remington," the man in the tractor roared. "You get back in that house until you're decent."

The woman made a face, pulled in her head and slammed down the window.

The man climbed down from the tractor and glared at J.J. "As for you, young lady, I don't know who the heck you are, but my boy wanted you stopped so I—"

"Be quiet." J.J. had registered the hazel eyes.

The man stood ramrod straight. "What did you say?"

"I said be quiet. I don't care if you're a general or—or an admiral or whatever, you can't come marching in here and call Luke a boy. He doesn't have to prove he's a man by going around shouting at people until he makes their heads ache, and he doesn't have to polish stupid little medals or march around in army boots or try to browbeat people just because he's some dinky little general. He—" A gloved hand pressed firmly over her mouth cut off J.J.'s diatribe.

"Be grateful O'Brien doesn't have any elk antlers handy," Luke said. "In her hands, they're lethal weapons."

J.J. shoved aside his hand. "I'm sick of hearing about those antlers." And even sicker at having jumped to Luke's defense.

"She's a beauty," General Remington reluctantly acknowledged, "but if she were my wife, I'd have her doing push-ups until she learned a little respect."

The woman who'd been stacking hay laughed as she walked up. "Luke, I think you better get your wife away from your father before she punches his lights out. Dad and Sara and I can feed the cattle. As for you, Lucius Remington, behave yourself. Just remember, you might have two stars, but I have three."

"You have three..." J.J. couldn't take it all in. Too many people, too many emotions, too many things she understood nothing about. Taking one embittered look at her car firmly embedded in a bank of snow, she started toward the gate.

"Where are you going?" Luke easily kept pace with her.

"Denver." She refused to look at him.

"Damn it, O'Brien, would you stop for one second? Mom said you came tearing down the road as if you were in the Indianapolis 500, you ran into the house and right back out again. Why didn't you stop when I yelled at you? What the hell is going on?''

She spun around to stand toe-to-toe with him. ''I returned the painting. That's what's going on.'' No way she'd tell him of the thousand and one emotions churning within her. Or of the jealous rage brought on by the sight of his sister. He and Sara could share a good laugh about that.

Luke grabbed her shoulders before she could take off again. ''You brought back the painting?'' he asked blankly. ''Why?''

''You know why.'' He could play the innocent all he wanted, but he wasn't fooling her. J.J. knocked aside his hands and headed down the road. Snow filled her shoes and clung to her stockings. Her feet felt like solid ice. Or they would have if she had any feeling left in them. Too bad her heart couldn't be iced down.

Her emotions had yo-yoed from jealous despair at the sight of a half-naked woman in Luke's house to giddy relief upon hearing the woman was his sister. All because of a man who didn't love her. The painting proved that. Outrage at the sneering message had served as an anesthetic partially blocking her pain, but now pain overrode her anger. J.J. wanted desperately to get home and lick her wounds.

Luke caught her arm. ''Would you stop running away?''

She wrenched out of his grasp. ''I'm not running, I'm walking away.''

''The hell you are.'' Luke scooped her up into his arms and retraced their steps toward his house.

She kicked wildly to break free. ''Put me down, or I'll—''

''Attack me with elk antlers?'' Hindered by the awkward, writhing burden held to his chest, Luke failed to see the patch of ice. His foot slid out from under him.

Feeling Luke totter, J.J. shrieked and grabbed his

neck, burying her face in his shoulder. Her abrupt movement proved too much for Luke's precarious balance. They toppled to the ground, J.J. landing half on Luke's body and half on a pile of warm, brown dirt. A foul odor engulfed her. Not dirt. "No, no, no!" she wailed, pummeling Luke's arm with her fists. Her blows bounced harmlessly off his sheepskin coat.

Luke jumped to his feet. "I think we've been down this road before." His eyes gleamed with suppressed laughter.

J.J. stood, ignoring the hand held out to help her up. "Since I met you, I've been pushed around, mauled by a psychopath, snowbound, attacked by vicious animals, coerced into delivering a baby, held at gunpoint, and driven into a snowbank, not once but twice." She added savagely, "Obviously I'm a slow learner."

"If you want me to apologize, I—"

"I want you to get out of my life." She'd give anything to exit on that line, but a passing breeze emphatically reminded her of her present condition. "I'm going in the house to take a shower and get dressed in whatever I find that halfway fits me. Then I'm going home. In my car. Because you and that crazy general you call your father are going to pull it out of the snowbank immediately." She spoke coldly to his right ear. "I'm going to replace all these clothes with new ones, and you will receive the bills for them." She started for the house.

"I know you're a little upset right now, J.J., but you'll feel better after a shower. Then we can talk." Luke spoke in the reasonable, patient tones of an adult attempting to cajole an unreasonable child out of a bad humor.

J.J. didn't stop to think. Spinning around, she shoved Luke as hard as she could. Her action took him totally by surprise, and he fell backward, his face a study in astonishment as he landed in a soft, brown pile. J.J.

stomped across the yard and into the house, passing Luke's sister without a word.

Slamming the bathroom door, J.J. wrestled open the window and tossed out every single item of clothing from her body. A lone, deciduous bush grew beneath the window. The heavier items plummeted through the bare branches to bury themselves in the snow. The top branches snagged her underwear. Pale pink silk waved in the breezes.

She took her time in the shower, filling the bathroom with warm steam and hoping she was inconveniencing every single, infuriating member of the Remington family. She had not the slightest shred of compunction about conscripting the female soap and sundries arrayed beside the sink. When the water finally ran cool, and every square inch of her body had been scrubbed practically raw, J.J. turned off the shower and stepped from the tub. Wrapping towels around her hair and body, she headed for Luke's room to pilfer his wardrobe.

Luke lay stretched out on his bed. His damp hair told J.J. he'd used the basement shower. Ignoring him and the traitorous lurch in her stomach, she ransacked his dresser drawers until she found a sweatshirt and sweatpants. Luke watched her in the mirror over the dresser. She scowled at him. "Get out. I want to get dressed."

"I won't see anything I haven't seen before."

Her fingers dug convulsively into the soft clothing. Moving one of those stupid cows would be easier than budging Luke. J.J. marched across the room, snatched his cowboy hat off a bottom bedpost and slammed it over his face. "Don't even think about peeking," she snapped.

"I don't have to peek." The hat muffled his words. "Every square inch of you is branded on my eyelids."

Luke's words conjured up images too painful to remember. Ruthlessly shoving them aside, J.J. quickly shrugged into the borrowed clothes. She wanted more from Luke than desire. Her purse sat on the dresser. She yanked a comb through her hair and smeared lotion on her face, all the while using the mirror to keep an eye on Luke.

He shoved back his hat to study the painting now propped against the foot of the bed. "At the gallery opening, you stood in front of this so long, I thought—"

"You thought I should be like that poor woman. Uprooted, dragged out to the back of beyond, nothing but a drudge and someone to warm his bed and raise his kids."

Luke drew his brows together in a brooding frown. "Is that what you see when you look at her?"

"Never mind what I see. You see a woman who can only be happy if she's her husband's servant, his plaything, his possession. You sent me that painting to tell me that's how a real wife is supposed to be. Docile, compliant and subservient."

Luke stood up and strolled over to the bedroom door. His back to J.J., he said, "My parents have been happily married for over thirty years. I expected to model my marriage after theirs. I screwed up."

J.J. meticulously replaced her belongings in her purse. "We both screwed up. We wanted different things from marriage. Any idiot could have seen we were wrong for each other."

Luke crossed the room to lean against the wall next to the dresser. "We need to talk."

"I'm through talking." Escape was the only thing on her mind. The bedroom door wouldn't open.

"I locked it and took the key. You're not leaving until we talk."

J.J. gave the doorknob a vicious shake. The lock held. She slumped against the door, resting her forehead against the solid wood. "There's nothing left to talk about."

She couldn't imagine why Luke had locked her in the

bedroom with him. He knew he could persuade her into his bed. Did he intend to try to persuade her into staying married—on his terms? J.J. didn't know if she had the willpower to fight him. And herself. Her heart wanted J.J. to throw herself in Luke's arms and believe everything would somehow work out. Her brain urged her to run before it was too late. "Open the door, Luke," she said tightly.

Luke didn't move. "The first time I saw you, you were listening to a woman and taking notes," he said. "I was struck by your intensity and your empathy. Then I saw your mouth, and a desire to kiss that mouth hit me so hard, I barely listened to the man talking to me. I was scheming how to meet you when Carl noticed the horse acting up. Before I could warn you, the horse broke free. Afterward, I saw what I'd knocked you into and knew I'd never get to nibble on that bottom lip or get to press kisses on that sexy beauty mark."

The composed words were rubber bullets thudding painfully into her back. More proof Luke's only interest in her had been physical. "I should have known you wouldn't forget the beauty mark."

He wasn't through. "After I knocked you down, I expected hysterics. Instead I could almost see your brain clicking away, analyzing what had happened. Your total acceptance of the situation, my actions and the unpleasant consequences for you knocked me for a loop. I think I fell in love with you the second you started laughing."

"You fell in love with me?" Whatever she expected Luke to say, it wasn't this. Never this. Wondering if she'd heard him wrong, J.J. slowly turned, clinging to the doorknob behind her.

"I know what you're thinking. It was crazy. I knew nothing about you except you'd focused on the critical aspect of the incident and discarded the rest as irrelevant. Based on that, I decided I was going to marry you. I thought you were the type of woman who'd never sweat the small stuff. I was sure you wouldn't fuss if I couldn't get away for a weekend because of an emergency on the ranch, or if I used the kitchen to save baby calves. You wouldn't mind if our kids were covered with bandages and dirt as long as they were happy and healthy.''

''You never told me any of that,'' she managed to say.

Luke smiled ruefully. ''Would you have believed me if I told you I'd fallen in love in the blink of an eye? I barely believed it, and after you kicked me out, it was easy enough to persuade myself I'd been blindsided by a kissable mouth, that subconsciously I knew I'd fallen for a beautiful face and I'd given the owner of that face the qualities I wanted her to have.''

Hope fled like air from a collapsing balloon. ''Well,'' J.J. said in a voice that barely wavered, ''now you know I don't have those qualities.''

''The only thing I know is I'm a fool.'' Luke swung around so he faced the mirror. ''You know what I see in here? Ad Parker.''

''Ad Parker?'' She stared uncomprehendingly at the rigid veins in his neck.

''He wants to control Birdie, because he's afraid she'll leave him. Like I wanted you dependent on me. The very strength that attracted me, scared the hell out of me. You didn't need me.'' Luke turned back toward her. ''I apologize for all I've put you through,'' he said formally.

How could he not know she needed him? Needed him to accept her, to trust her. To love her. ''Yes, well, I guess, it's over,'' she stammered, hardly knowing what she was saying.

''I know that. Instead of tying you to me, I drove you away and into Alexander's arms. I can't change what's past, but I won't interfere in your life anymore.'' His voice held no inflection. ''You have my blessing on your marriage with Alexander. I'll sign whatever divorce papers you send.''

"I don't want your blessing." Luke's words failed to clear her muddled head. Why had he told her he'd once loved her, now when he seemed to be saying it was too late? Did Luke love her or not? If he'd given her even the slightest hint he loved her, that he no longer expected her to fit his rigid notions of a wife, that he wanted the kind of woman she was, J.J. would have dashed across the room and into his arms.

He said nothing.

J.J.'s self-restraint exploded. She'd begun to hope, and he'd flung those hopes in the same kind of barnyard piles he'd shoved her into. She dug in her purse for a pencil and notebook. "You'll find my pantsuit, coat and shoes outside. Brands and sizes are in them." Scribbling a few lines, she ripped off the top page and walked over to stick it into Luke's shirt pocket. "My sizes and favorite lingerie store. Burton likes sweet and girlish white lingerie with lots of lace and ruffles and bows."

"If Burton thinks you're sweet and girlish, he doesn't have a clue what makes you tick."

"Unlike you?" J.J. asked in an acid voice.

Luke stepped nearer until his body barely touched hers. "Unlike dumb cowboy me."

"You know nothing about me," J.J. managed to say. His body heat penetrated her fleece clothing and warmed her skin. Breathing filled her head with his scent.

Luke framed her face with his callused palms and stared down into her face. "I know everything I need to know about you," he said with quiet conviction. Dropping his hands, he dragged her across the room to stand in front of the dresser. He propped the watercolor against the mirror. "This is who you are."

J.J. lifted her eyes to Luke's face in the mirror and willed her mouth not to quiver. "She bears no resemblance to me."

"Not on the outside, no." His eyes captured J.J.'s in the mirror. "On the inside. You're both the type to face up to everything life throws at you. You fight fear to do what has to be done. Compliant? Subservient? Not this woman. She's as ready to defend her family as you were to defend Birdie.'' His voice altered subtly. ''And me.''

She knew what he referred to. ''I wasn't defending you,'' she quickly denied. ''Your father irritated me, is all.''

''When my dad calls me his boy, he does it with pride. A pride he made me earn, so it means something to both of us.''

Who cared about his stupid old father? Not J.J. Not when hope kept slipping back into her heart. ''He's as bossy and opinionated as you are. Your mother's life must be hell.''

Luke shrugged, dismissing her words. ''Every time Dad pins on new rank, Mom promotes herself. To remind him she's not about to take any guff from him.''

''I don't know how she stands him.''

''She loves him. And when you love someone...'' Laying down the painting, Luke turned J.J. to face him. A quizzical smile played across his mouth. ''You don't want my blessing. You returned the painting. A man has to give his wife something for a wedding present.''

Smiling wasn't fair. J.J.'s stomach turned triple flips. She fought the discombobulating sensation. ''Ex-wife,'' she managed to say.

The outer corners of his eyes crinkled. ''I guess I'll have to buy you lingerie.''

''You can't give me lingerie.''

''That's not what you said earlier.'' He tapped the piece of paper sticking out of his shirt pocket. ''You ordered lingerie, you'll get lingerie. No ruffles and bows and not white. Pink and blue and pale green and turquoise to match your eyes.'' He lightly skimmed her cheekbones with his thumbs.

''My eyes are aqua,'' she blurted out, holding her head still. Her skin tingled.

Luke ran a finger back and forth over her lower lip. "Aqua, then. Nightgowns and panties and those smooth, silky, slinky things I liked...?"

"Teddies," she muttered involuntarily. His every word acted as a physical caress. Desire shimmered over J.J.'s skin and surged through her veins. She fought to keep the increasing heat in his hazel eyes from melting her good sense. Did Luke think he could seduce her into becoming his kind of wife? "What do you want from me, Luke?"

"C'mon, O'Brien, figure it out. You're a lawyer."

A clump of snow in her face couldn't have cleared her head faster than Luke's taunting challenge. J.J. batted down Luke's hands and ducked under his arms. Darn him, she was a lawyer. A good one. One who'd had extensive dealings with reluctant witnesses. Luke Remington was going to tell her what kind of game he was playing, or she'd turn in her law degree.

J.J. knew from experience when direct questions didn't work, one used unconventional methods to dig out the truth. Putting a few feet between her and the arrogant cowboy who eyed her as if she were a prime steak, she said obliquely, "I suspect your pie-baker will be moving to Denver in the not too distant future."

Luke's eyes darkened with exasperation as he braced a hip against the dresser. "Susan and I are friends. Don't worry about her."

J.J. refrained from making an issue of his conceited assumption. "I'm not worried about her. She'll make Burton an excellent wife and Carrie a wonderful mother."

Luke abruptly rose to his full height. "Susan and Alexander? What does that mean?" His eyes narrowed. "You and Alexander aren't getting married?" Luke inhaled sharply when she shook her head. "And you didn't bother to let me know?"

"Why should I? What difference does it make to

you?'' She backed away at the predatory look on Luke's face.

"I'll tell you what difference it makes, O'Brien." He stalked her across the bedroom floor. "Not only am I retracting my blessing, but I'm refusing to sign any divorce papers."

"You can't do that. I refuse to stay married to a man who loves a stupid cardboard image of the perfect wife." The foot of the bed stopped her retreat. She inched slowly around it. "I want, I need, a husband who loves me—the me I am."

Luke's steps mirrored her every move. "How 'bout what I want?" he asked silkily, encircling her throat with his hand.

J.J. involuntarily stepped backward, stopping when she rammed into the side of the bed. "Wanting me isn't enough," she half whispered.

Luke moved his hands down to warm her breasts. "But I like wanting you." A heavy-lidded look of male satisfaction rode his face as her nipples hardened beneath fleece to push against his palms. "And I like you wanting me." His thumbs brushed against sensitive tips.

"I don't." J.J. jerked back, away from his mind-numbing touch. The bed caught her behind her knees, and she toppled backward.

Luke followed her down, pinning her to the mattress with his long, hard body. "You want me, so you must mean you don't like it." He smoothed her hair back from her face. "Why not?"

"You don't love me," J.J. said bleakly.

"Don't tell me who I love or don't love, lawyer lady." Luke fiercely gripped her head, his eyes blazing down at her. "I love the way you stride through life. I love the way you do what you have to do, whether it's tough or inconvenient or frightening. I love your independence. I love your bimbo mouth and your sexy beauty mark, but mostly I love that damned defiant chin.

I love everything about you," he said in a harsh voice, raw with need, "but say the words, and I'm out of your life forever."

"What words?" Her heart pounded in her throat.

"Tell me you don't love me."

J.J. swallowed. "I can't. I never could."

Relief swept across Luke's face, chased away by a look loaded with triumph and sexy male complacency. "That better mean you intend to stick with a slow-learning cowboy. I have Ethel to clean and cook, and Jeff and Dale to help on the ranch, but I need a woman to love me." He warmed her cheeks with his palms, his thumbs resting against the corners of her mouth. "A special woman. A capable, independent, mouthy, strong lawyer lady." He smiled lazily, sure of himself now. Sure of her. "That doesn't mean I won't try to persuade you to practice law here instead of in Denver."

J.J. could have told him then she'd resigned from the Denver firm. Instead she gave him a look from under lowered lashes. "How did you plan to go about that, cowboy?"

"I bought an office building in town," he muttered against her lips.

J.J. froze, then, with an enormous heave, she pushed him off her. He landed on his back beside her. "You bought a building?" she asked in a deadly calm voice. "The insurance office?" At Luke's nod, she thrust her face down to his. "Who appointed you to make my decisions?"

"I'm not trying to run your life," Luke said carefully. "If you want to stay with the law firm in Denver, I'll support your decision."

J.J. eyed him doubtfully. "You wouldn't care if I lived in Denver and we only saw each other on weekends?"

"I'd care, but I'd accept it. I love you, O'Brien. I want you to be happy. I'd be happier if you practiced law closer to home, but I didn't buy the building to force you into quitting the Denver firm. If you don't want the office, I'll rent it to someone else.''

"And that would be the end of it?"

"Absolutely." Luke pulled her over on top of him.

"Liar." J.J. pinned a scowl on her face. "You know very well you intend to nag and bully me until you get your own way."

He widened his eyes in astonishment at her accusation. "I'd never bully you." One corner of his mouth twitched. "I might try a little bribery. Generous rental terms for the office."

J.J. gave him a suspicious look. "How generous?"

Luke laughed softly, tugging her head downward. "Free rent," he said against her mouth, "in exchange for giving your beauty mark to all our daughters."

"Daughters, yes." She helped Luke pull the sweatshirt over her head. "Beauty mark, no." Laughter puffed warmly against her breast. "I'm serious, Luke. You cannot change my mind." She wondered how the beauty mark would look with hazel eyes.

"I'll bronze the elk antlers." He slid his hands beneath her waistband. "They'd look great over your desk."

J.J. knew he didn't mean over her desk in Denver. "Give me one good reason why I should move out here to the boonies."

He gave her more than one. All very good ones.

AUTHOR NOTE

There are over fifty areas of thermal activity in Colorado, but I don't know of any hot springs in North Park. If you want to tell Luke Remington he can't have a hot spring pool on his ranch, be my guest.

HARLEQUIN WOMEN KNOW ROMANCE WHEN THEY SEE IT.

And they'll see it on **ROMANCE CLASSICS**, the new 24-hour TV channel devoted to romantic movies and original programs like the special **Harlequin® Showcase of Authors & Stories.**

The **Harlequin® Showcase of Authors & Stories** introduces you to many of your favorite romance authors in a program developed exclusively for Harlequin® readers.

Watch for the **Harlequin® Showcase of Authors & Stories** series beginning in the summer of 1997.

ROMANCE CLASSICS

*If you're not receiving **ROMANCE CLASSICS**, call your local cable operator or satellite provider and ask for it today!*

Escape to the network of your dreams.

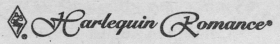
Harlequin Romance

is pleased to offer

SIMPLY THE BEST

*Authors you'll treasure,
books you'll want to keep!*

These are romances we know you'll love reading—
over and over again! Because they are,
quite simply, the best....

Watch for these special books by some of your
favorite authors:

#3468 WILD AT HEART
by Susan Fox (August 1997)

#3471 DO YOU TAKE THIS COWBOY?
by Jeanne Allan (September 1997)

#3477 NO WIFE REQUIRED!
by Rebecca Winters (October 1997)

Available in August, September and October 1997
wherever Harlequin books are sold.

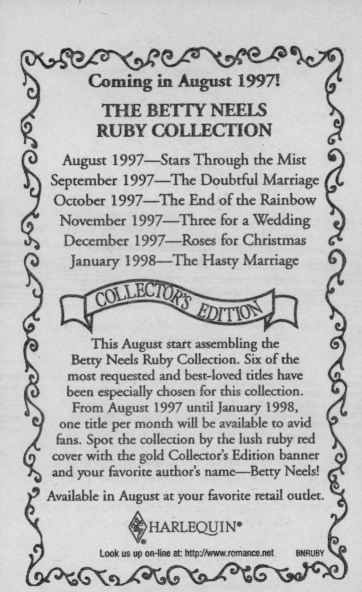

Coming in August 1997!

THE BETTY NEELS
RUBY COLLECTION

COLLECTOR'S EDITION

This August start assembling the
Betty Neels Ruby Collection. Six of the
most requested and best-loved titles have
been especially chosen for this collection.
From August 1997 until January 1998,
one title per month will be available to avid
fans. Spot the collection by the lush ruby red
cover with the gold Collector's Edition banner
and your favorite author's name—Betty Neels!

Available in August at your favorite retail outlet.

◆ HARLEQUIN®

Let's Celebrate!

LOVE & LAUGHTER™

invites you to the party of the season!

Grab your popcorn and be prepared to laugh as we celebrate with **LOVE & LAUGHTER**.

Harlequin's newest series is going Hollywood!

Let us make you laugh with three months of terrific books, authors and romance, plus a chance to win a FREE 15-copy video collection of the best romantic comedies ever made.

For more details look in the back pages of any Love & Laughter title, from July to September, at your favorite retail outlet.

Don't forget the popcorn!

Available wherever
Harlequin books are sold.

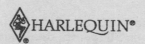 HARLEQUIN®

LLCELEB